D0329246

LACEY'S HOMECOMING

Other books by Rosemarie Naramore

Armed and Disarming
The Detour
Just in Time
The Listing Agent

LACEY'S HOMECOMING

•

Rosemarie Naramore

AVALON BOOKS
NEW YORK

Published by Avalon Books,
an imprint of Thomas Bouregy & Co., Inc.
160 Madison Avenue, New York, NY 10016

Library of Congress Cataloging-in-Publication Data

Naramore, Rosemarie.
  Lacey's homecoming / Rosemarie Naramore.
      p. cm.
  ISBN 978-0-8034-7604-2 (hardcover)
  I. Title.
  PS3614.A685L33 2011
  813'.6—dc22

                              2011018708

PRINTED IN THE UNITED STATES OF AMERICA
ON ACID-FREE PAPER
BY RR DONNELLEY, BLOOMSBURG, PENNSYLVANIA

For my sister, Martha

Chapter One

Lacey's eyes fluttered open. She struggled to focus. Was that a face in front of her? She reached a tentative hand toward it but just didn't have the strength, and her hand dropped to the bed. She blinked over and over again until finally the face grew incrementally less fuzzy.

A man's face? An angel's face? With his wavy chestnut hair, compassionate hazel eyes with golden flecks, perfectly straight nose over full, masculine lips—indeed, an angel. But she couldn't be sure. Still too fuzzy.

She tried to move. Ouch. It hurt to move. She moaned.

"Lacey?" The face moved closer.

Yes. An angel.

The face moved closer still. She fought to focus, to get a good look at that angel. *Oh, heaven must be lovely,* she thought, *if all the angels look like this one.* And then, finally, her vision cleared. Her eyes widened. She knew that face. "Ah, heck," she said dazedly, "I'm in hell."

She heard the man's throaty chuckle as she drifted off to blessed sleep.

"Is she awake? *Really* awake this time?"

Lacey heard the question and recognized the voice. Lord, it was Mason James. What was he doing here? What was *she* doing here?

Once again, her eyes fluttered open. She glanced around

1

the room, recognized it as a hospital room, and then turned to the source of the voice. It was Mason James all right, standing beside her bed, a concerned smile creasing his face.

"'Bout time you woke up," he said. "You had us worried, Lacey Jane."

"Lacey," she corrected him. She'd long ago dropped the *Jane.* "What happened?"

"You've been in an accident."

"What?" she said dazedly.

He sighed heavily. "Apparently, you were driving into town Tuesday night. You were stopped on Main Street and . . ."

"And what?" she asked shakily.

He winced. "You were T-boned, by a couple of drunk kids."

She shook her head, tried to remember. She caught his gaze. A piercing pain sliced through her head, causing her to squeeze her eyelids shut. She raised a trembling hand to her forehead and pressed, as if attempting to force the pain away.

"You're hurting? She's hurting." Mason beckoned to a nurse who stood in the doorway. "She's in a lot of pain," he said worriedly. "Can you give her something?"

She opened her eyes and saw the nurse. The young woman quickly scooted around the bed, taking up a vigil at the other side.

"I'm okay," Lacey said, although she didn't particularly believe it herself. She felt stiff, uncomfortable, and attempted to shift her body. Her eyes widened in terror when she couldn't manage to move her lower extremities. She struggled to sit up, but couldn't muster the strength. Apparently, Mason read the fear in her eyes, and he gently took ahold of her shoulders.

"Don't move," he soothed. "You're going to be fine."

"I *can't* move!" she said shrilly. "Am I . . . ?"

He smiled reassuringly. "No, you're not paralyzed. You do have a badly broken leg, and it's currently being held together by so much hardware, it's understandable you don't have the strength to lift it."

"I don't . . ."

"You don't remember," the nurse said softly. "It's to be expected. You sustained a blow to your head and have a concussion. No need to worry," she added quickly. "Many trauma patients are unable to recollect the details of a serious accident. Many never recall the actual impact."

Just the same, she struggled to remember. She tried to remember sitting at the light at Main Street, but couldn't recall having been there. She was relieved to realize she remembered the drive from Portland to Westover, but Tuesday night . . . It was a blur.

She glanced at Mason. "What day is it?"

"It's Friday."

"I've been out of it for three days?" she murmured.

He nodded. "Yes. But the doctor tells me you're definitely on the mend now."

Suddenly, she remembered why she'd driven to Westover in the first place—what had prompted her to leave Portland in such a rush. Grandma. Grandma Rennie was horribly ill. She had had a massive stroke late Tuesday afternoon.

Lacey had received the call while she'd been at work, in the process of cleaning out her desk in readiness for her impending move to Westover. She'd dropped everything and left for her hometown that very moment. Her exit interview with human resources would simply have to wait.

She knew she'd have to return soon, to dot her i's and cross her t's at work, but she'd already seen to most of the other details relating to the upcoming move. She'd sold her condo—such a relief—and had stored the bulk of her possessions in a pay-by-the-month storage unit. She intended to retrieve any needed items later, but knew she'd likely sell many of her things. The bare essentials were already stored in the trunk of her economy car—or had been. Now, who knew? But her other things, well, Rennie's house was small, and already filled with so many personal mementos there wasn't room for much else.

Lacey had made the decision to move to Westover a month before, due to her grandmother's failing health. She had been ill for several months and had had a series of mini-strokes that had slowed her down but hadn't incapacitated her fully. Just the same, she knew Rennie needed her, although she would never impose on her by asking for help. She was independent— had always been independent and would be independent to her dying day.

A phone conversation with her grandmother's doctor had convinced her that Rennie could no longer live alone. When Rennie had scoffed at the notion of moving to Portland with her—just as Lacey had known she would—Lacey had proposed the only other solution. She would move to Westover. She hadn't planned to officially move into her grandmother's home until Saturday—tomorrow—but the events of Tuesday night had assuredly altered her plans.

"Grandma!" Lacey cried suddenly.

If Rennie had had her stroke Tuesday, where was she now? Was she in this hospital too?

Mason didn't immediately speak, but he shot a worried glance at the nurse. The young woman nodded and turned her eyes to Lacey, as if bracing for . . .

What? Lacey wondered. Why was the nurse watching her so sympathetically?

She attempted to sit up again but couldn't manage it. She winced with frustration. "How is my grandmother? I received a call at work Tuesday. I was told she had a stroke. Is she here at the hospital? I have to see her."

Mason sighed heavily and took her hand. She met his eyes,

and he held her gaze as he delivered the awful news. "Rennie passed late Tuesday night."

She watched him in abject horror. She shook her head. This was a dream. Yes, a dream. No . . . a nightmare. She couldn't find the words to vocalize her thoughts. Surely, this was a nightmare.

"Lacey," he prompted softly. "Honey . . ."

"No, it can't be." She shook her head. "I came to see her." Her eyes widened. She attempted to pull her hand away from him, but he held firm. "I didn't say good-bye. No, this can't be real."

She began to cry, unable to hold back the tears, despite the fact that she never cried. Lacey Karr never cried. Not Lacey Karr, formerly of Westover, Oregon, granddaughter of Texanna Irenda "Rennie" Karr and daughter of Jessie Karr.

Lacey had never known her mother, Jessie, or her father. In fact, she didn't even know her father's name. Thanks to Jessie, she had lived under the specter of ongoing speculation while in Westover—had struggled to hold her head up high when the eyes of the town were on her and the weight of the world had been squarely on her shoulders. It was because of Jessie that she had hightailed it out of Westover as fast as her legs would take her after she'd graduated from high school.

"Lacey," Mason said softly.

She shook her head to clear it of memories better forgotten for now. "Was Grandma . . . alone?" she asked, steeling herself for his answer. The thought that Rennie had died alone was almost too much to bear. Oh, why hadn't she made the move sooner?

"No," he said, his deep voice kind and firm. "No, Dad was with her. She went peacefully. He said as peacefully as he's ever seen a person go. Lacey, she was ready."

"Were you with her too?"

"No, I was with you."

She nodded, forgetting her physical pain. The pain in her broken body could never compare to the pain in her broken heart.

Lacey woke early the next morning. Her head wasn't nearly as foggy as it had been, and she searched her brain for some bit of elusive something she couldn't quite remember. And then it hit her. Her grandmother was dead. She had had a massive stroke. And Lacey hadn't arrived in time to see her, since she'd been in an accident.

Once again, she felt a wave of guilt at the realization that she hadn't been with Rennie when she passed, but then she forced herself to come to terms with that reality. She knew her grandmother wouldn't have had time for such nonsense, would have told her in no uncertain terms that any guilt was a waste of time and effort.

Rennie would have said, "Lacey Jane, I know how much you love me. I know. I died knowing, so don't you be spending your time feeling bad about anything."

Suddenly, she saw her grandmother's sweet face in her mind's eye and heard her voice once again. "We'll see each other again, Lacey girl. You know that. And you *know* how I feel about good-byes. . . ."

No, Grandma wasn't big on good-byes. In her lifetime, people who said good-bye rarely came back. . . .

Lacey attempted to raise her upper body in the bed, but she just couldn't manage it. She reached a tentative hand to her head and gingerly explored the lump on her forehead. It hurt, but she knew she'd live. When her hand felt the rough texture of her usually sleek blond hair, she sighed.

"Your hair is your crowning glory, Lacey girl," Rennie used to say. "And you have hair like a princess."

She had always laughed at that. Even at a tender age, she

knew princesses were the stuff of fairy tales, and her life was certainly no fairy tale.

She knew there wasn't anything regal about her hair—and certainly not about her heritage. She'd grown up on the other side of the tracks, with a grandmother who could barely make ends meet. No, she wasn't a fairy princess, but she was loved. She hadn't ever wanted for love. Rennie had seen to that.

She felt the tears spring to her eyes. She wiped them away just as a nurse entered the room. This wasn't the same woman from last night, but was instead older and well padded around her middle. She wore her dark hair in a tight bun on her head, and though the style was severe, there was nothing severe about her compassionate brown eyes.

"How are we feeling today?" the nurse asked. She must have noticed Lacey's hand doing an exploration of her filthy hair. She patted her arm. "I'm Millie," she said. "Now listen, I don't want you worrying about your hair, honey. The doctor had to trim some away to stitch up a cut at the back of your head, but he was careful. Only cut off what he had to."

Her eyes widened. She hadn't realized she'd sustained a blow to the back of her head as well. The lump on her forehead seemed to be the source of her head pain.

"You have beautiful hair," the nurse gushed. "You don't often see that shade of blond. And it's real."

"How can you tell?" Lacey rarely gave much thought to her hair, or looks, for that matter.

"Nobody could touch up the roots that well," she said with a grin. "So, how are we feeling today?"

She shook her head. How was she feeling? Before she could answer, the nurse spoke for her. "You're feeling stiff, groggy, and shell-shocked." She patted her hand. "I'm so sorry about your grandmother. I know you've been through a lot these last several days."

She nodded numbly. "Thank you."

"Well," Millie chirped brightly, "I know how we can make you feel better."

Lacey watched her quizzically.

"We're going to wash your hair. We'll have to be careful, of course, but we'll get it done. I know I always feel better when my hair is clean and combed."

She had to concede her hair was probably her finest feature, since it remained a shiny, platinum blond despite that she was now an adult of twenty-nine. It hadn't dulled or darkened as happened to most blonds, which surprised her as much as anyone. Her complexion was golden rather than pink, and there wasn't a single freckle to be found on her upturned nose. Her lips, however, were both pink and full.

Today, after days in a hospital bed, she could only imagine how awful she must look. She suspected her face was sorely lacking color.

"I'll just check your blood pressure, and we'll get that hair washed," the nurse said.

In no time, Millie had efficiently washed her hair, somehow managing to keep both her and the bed dry in the process. "I'm not quite sure how you managed that," Lacey said, after the nurse passed her a mirror.

"Practice," Millie said crisply, and then stood back. "Well, now, won't you be looking pretty for your young man?"

"Wha—?" she said, eyeing the woman curiously. What young man? Had Keith heard about her accident? Not that he was her young man. But had he come to Westover? If so, where was he now?

"Sheriff James has hardly left your side," Millie said with a crisp shake of her head.

She shook her head confusedly. "Mason?"

"He was first to the scene of your accident." She leaned in and whispered, "I hear from other rescue personnel he was beside himself." She shook her head in wonder. "Just so you know, he *never* falls apart. He's a tower of strength, that one. Cool . . . as . . . a . . . cucumber."

The nurse began tugging at the bed covers and neatly tucked them around Lacey. She glanced up and nodded her head in measured intervals. "I guess one of his deputies had to restrain him when the firefighters were using the Jaws of Life to cut you out of your car."

Lacey opened her mouth to speak. She couldn't find any words.

"He must really love you," Millie said.

Yeah, right. Mason James, love her? She would have laughed out loud if she'd had any humor left in her. Back in the day, he had been the bane of her existence. He had been her nemesis, her arch rival, and a colossal pain in her backside. And the truth was, she had been the female equivalent of all of the above—to him.

Mason James in love with her? Sure. When hell froze over.

Chapter Two

It's about time we got you out of this hospital, Lacey." Dr. Sandison lowered the chart and smiled. "You're doing so well, there's little more we can do for you here."

She attempted a smile in return. She was grateful for the care she had received and continued to receive at the hospital, but she still couldn't wrap her mind around her having been in a serious collision that had prevented her from seeing her grandmother one last time before she passed.

Adding insult to injury was the realization that she had a badly broken leg, and according to Dr. Sandison, her orthopedic surgeon had said she would need a wheelchair for mobility over the upcoming several weeks, if not months. Thankfully, the head injury hadn't caused permanent damage, and she counted herself fortunate for that.

"What are your plans?" Dr. Sandison asked, jolting her from her thoughts. He reached out to gently pat the foot on her leg that wasn't enclosed in a cast. It was a fatherly gesture from a man who had known her since she was a little girl.

She sighed loudly in response to his question. "I . . . guess I'll stay at Grandma's house."

The doctor promptly shook his head. "There's no way you can be alone right now. Aside from the obvious logistical problems—all those steps—you're going to need help with just about everything."

"I'll be fine," she assured him. "I'm sure I'd do fine with crutches. . . ."

He shook his head adamantly. "You'll use a wheelchair," he said in a tone that defied argument. "Look, that leg is in a precarious state. According to Dr. Marks, your orthopedist, those pins cannot—and I repeat—cannot move a fraction, or you could do serious damage to the work he's done—not to mention your leg," he added. "Unless you're willing to risk a second surgery, then I suggest you listen to me."

She sighed again. "How long until I can use crutches, then?"

"We can't say just yet," he told her. "It'll depend on how well you heal. Dr. Marks will be able to give you a better idea in a few weeks."

She raised a hand to her forehead, since she felt the beginnings of a headache. What was she going to do? She could have returned to Portland and stayed with a good friend, Laura, but her friend was currently vacationing in Hawaii. She wasn't scheduled to return for ten days. She was certain Laura would drive from Portland to retrieve her just as soon as she returned, but until then . . .

"Well?" he prompted.

"Maybe I can stay with Donna . . . ," she mused, and quickly dismissed the idea. "No, no, I can't do that. She has enough on her plate."

"Three little kids, and one on the way," Dr. Sandison said. "I pray she and Chet get that little girl they're so desperate for."

"Me, too," she said distractedly. She knew full well she couldn't impose on Donna. Aside from the fact that Donna had a full house, she hadn't kept in regular contact with her former best friend. When she had left Westover, she hadn't looked back—other than to stay in touch with her grandma. She suspected she had hurt Donna's feelings, though she hadn't intended to. It had simply been easier to put Westover in the past.

"Martha and I would take you in," he said, "but we just don't have the room now. Did I tell you we sold the old place?"

She nodded. He had mentioned that he and Martha had bought a condo by the lake. They had decided to downsize when the last of their three children finished college.

"I wouldn't have imposed, anyway," she assured him.

"Lacey, Lacey, Lacey, it wouldn't have been an imposition," he said sternly. "Martha would have loved having you and so would I. She still reminisces about you, five years old in Sunday school class and so full of questions. She got such a kick out of your inquisitive nature."

"That's one way to describe it," she muttered.

She had been inquisitive, but she was certain most of the church congregation hadn't found that quality the least bit endearing. Intrusive, boorish, obnoxious, but certainly not endearing.

"Remember when—" Dr. Sandison began, but she silenced him with a hand.

"Please, don't remind me," she begged.

"Okay, okay." He chuckled. "I won't remind you, but I still can't help but laugh when I remember you that one time standing up in front of that church and—"

"Please," she moaned. "I still can't stand to think about it."

"Oh, Lacey, you were just a baby. Had barely started kindergarten and—"

She shook her head vigorously. She didn't want to think about her early years in Westover. She didn't like to think about her years in Westover at all. She was almost grateful when Mason strode into the room, whistling a tune.

"Hey, doc. How's our patient today?" he inquired, smiling. "Behaving herself?"

"She's been a model patient."

"I don't believe it," he said, cocking his head to the side and pretending to study her with a critical eye. "Frankly, I'm surprised you haven't had to resort to restraints to keep her down."

Lacey indicated the cast on her leg with a chagrined nod. The leg was presently dangling from a metal contraption high above the bed. "I have no choice but to be a model patient. I'm in traction."

"Effective," he mused.

"Lacey and I were just discussing her impending release from the hospital," Dr. Sandison said cheerfully. "We're just not sure where she's headed—"

"To my house," Mason cut in.

Her eyes snapped to his face. *"What?"*

"Excellent," Dr. Sandison enthused, before she could get another word in. "I don't think I could have released her in good conscience if I hadn't known she was off to a safe location."

Lacey struggled to sit more upright in the bed. "Uh, Mason, while I appreciate your offer, I can't take you up on it." She turned to the doctor. "Isn't there some care facility I could stay at, just until my friend gets back from a trip to—"

"Why would you want to do that?" Mason asked, his hands on his hips. He watched her as if she'd taken leave of her senses, and then turned to the doctor. "Are you releasing her today?"

"Tomorrow," he said, "now that we know she has a place to go."

She shook her head adamantly. "Again, while I appreciate your offer—"

"If I remember right, you have a master on your main floor," the doctor directed to Mason, effectively cutting her off. "Didn't the former owners add on the master suite for a disabled parent? An elderly mother, right?"

"Right. The bathroom is wheelchair accessible and even has a shower that can accommodate a wheelchair."

"Good, good," the doctor said. "It'll be so much easier for her with the appropriate accommodations."

"Now, wait just a minute," she said, glancing from the doctor to Mason. "Like I said, I really appreciate the offer of a place to stay, but I'll be staying at my grandma's place. . . ."

"Independent little cuss," Dr. Sandison said affectionately. "You were always such a tough little thing." He turned to Mason, ignoring her altogether now. "I remember one time she fell out of a tree and broke her arm. Broke it clean through. Didn't even cry." He shook his head ruefully. "If memory serves, Tommy Hall pushed her out of that tree and she just wouldn't give him the satisfaction of shedding a tear."

The doctor gave Mason an assessing glance. "And if memory serves, you made sure ol' Tommy did some crying himself when you found out what he'd done to her."

She felt a wave of mortification wash over her. Indeed, when Mason had seen the cast on her arm and discovered Tommy was responsible, he had taken out after Tommy like a coon dog on a scent. She had been appalled when she'd heard about Tommy's black eye. She'd been eight at the time and fully capable of fighting her own battles. In fact, she'd soon taken out after Tommy herself and had made good use of her cast when she'd struck him hard on the mouth, adding insult to his already injured face.

Dr. Sandison chuckled again. "Lacey, Lacey, Lacey," he murmured. "If you weren't sporting a cast, you were covered with poison ivy or bee stings. Just couldn't keep you out of mischief."

Mason laughed. "Remember the time . . ."

His words trailed when Lacey desperately struggled to prop her upper body up on her elbows, but she didn't quite have the strength. She fell back against the pillow—hard.

"Careful," Mason cautioned, studying her tense features. He could see by the hard set of her jaw that she wasn't interested in a stroll down memory lane. "We'd better stop, Doc," he said. "When that cast comes off, she's liable to extract a little revenge on *us*."

The doctor made a mock-frightened face, and she slumped even further into her pillow. "I'm past my vendetta phase. I don't extract revenge on anyone—anymore." She shifted in the bed slightly and felt a piercing pain stab her lower back.

"Your occupation as lawyer fills that need now, huh?" Mason said, biting back a chuckle.

"Funny," she muttered, struggling to reach her aching back.

"Feeling some pain, Lacey?" the doctor asked with concern.

"Just stiffening up from all the time in this bed. I really need to get out of here."

"Tomorrow!" he said cheerfully, and then consulted his watch. "I have another patient to see now, but I'll be sure to stop by and check on you before I leave for the day."

She attempted a grateful smile as he left the room.

"So you'll be a free woman tomorrow," Mason observed as he dropped into the chair beside her bed.

"Look, again, while I appreciate your offer . . ."

He bit back a smile. "Look, Lacey Jane, the way I see it, you don't have many options. Tell me, if not to my house, then where do you plan to go?"

"Like I told Doc Sandison, to Grandma's," she said impatiently.

He shook his head. "You're stuck in a wheelchair, whether

you like it or not. You're not going to be able to get around, let alone get yourself in and out of bed. And then there's the problem of bathing and using the—"

"Okay, I get your meaning," she assured him wearily, but then brightened. "Wait, no, I should be fine at Grandma's. There's a bathroom on the main floor and I can sleep on the couch." Her formerly pale face suddenly shone with rosy anticipation. "It'll work!" she declared.

"Lacey, Lacey, Lacey," he intoned.

"Why must you people always use my name in triplicate?" she muttered, frustrated.

"You know why, Lacey Jane. You've always been as stubborn as the day is long."

"Stubborn?" she enunciated carefully. "You don't know anything about me."

"And whose fault is that? You're the one who raced out of this town so fast you left our heads spinning."

"So? Isn't that what most adults do? Strike out on their own? Make their own way in the world?"

He shrugged. "Sure, but many people I know retain a healthy fondness for the old hometown. Ever hear of a telephone?"

She ignored the telephone remark. "Don't they say, 'You can't go home again'?"

"You can if you want to. We missed you."

The words spoken with sincerity caused a warm glow to stain her cheeks. He missed her? Really?

Not likely.

She sighed loudly. "Look, I don't want to argue with you about all this, and I certainly don't want to impose on you. You have a life, for Pete's sake."

He leaned forward in the chair and clasped his hands together. "I'm happy to have you stay with me. It's the only solution, as far as I can see. And frankly, I don't understand why you're so resistant to the idea. We grew up together—practically spent every summer day together growing up."

"Yeah, well, if memory serves, it was that very reality that prompted you to declare me a colossal pain in your butt."

"We're adults now," he said with a twinkle in his eye. "And . . . it remains to be seen whether or not you're a colossal pain in anyone's butt these days. But then again, you are a lawyer. . . ."

She made a face, but managed to fight the impulse to stick out her tongue at him. "So you know, you were the pain—and you were more of an allover pain, Mr. High and Mighty Mason James. . . ."

"Hey, now you're just being mean," he interrupted. "I was protective, that's all. And Lord knows you needed protecting," he added with a chagrined smile. "I remember the time—"

"Stop!" she commanded.

He raised a hand in surrender, grinned, and sat back in the chair and folded his hands behind his head. He watched her speculatively, causing her to shift uncomfortably beneath his penetrating gaze. Having his eyes pinned on her face with such intensity caused her heart to give an erratic thump.

He had always been good-looking, but now, as an adult of thirty-two, he was drop-dead gorgeous—the embodiment of masculinity in a law enforcement uniform. Too bad he was Mason James.

"It *has* been a long time, Lacey Jane," he drawled.

"Not long enough," she muttered.

He chuckled. "Don't know why, but I have always rubbed you the wrong way, haven't I?"

She gave a snort. "I'd say it was the other way around."

"You never rubbed me the wrong way. In fact . . ."

The words hung in the air, since a nurse appeared in the room, carrying a dinner tray. She deftly pressed a button to raise the bed, gently lowered Lacey's leg, and then placed the food in front of her, which proved an awkward maneuver, since she didn't take her eyes off Mason during the exchange.

He simply smiled lazily, as if he wasn't aware that the woman nearly dumped a plate of chicken breast and mashed potatoes onto Lacey's lap. When the nurse left the room with a backward mournful glance at him, Lacey rolled her eyes.

"Still have a way with the ladies, I see," she said drolly.

He feigned a stricken look. "I have no idea what you're talking about. I've always been the shy and retiring type."

"Ugly too," she remarked.

He didn't even flinch, but laughed instead. "Aren't you going to eat anything?" he asked, pointing at the tray in front of her.

She shrugged. "I'm not very hungry. Why, do you want it?"

"No! I don't want it. I could smuggle in a pizza, if that sounds more appetizing."

She shook her head, although the prospect of a pizza was more appealing. "About my living arrangements," she began again, but this time he raised a silencing hand.

"It's settled. We're going to be roommates, Lacey Jane—at least until you're on the mend."

Chapter Three

The next morning, Mason rolled Lacey up the newly installed ramp to the front porch and into the wide foyer of his home. She had been surprised by the grandeur of the house, which sat on tree-lined acreage just outside of town. Several other large homes occupied parcels of nearby land in an upscale development called Deer Run Woods.

"How long have you lived here?" she inquired, glancing around. The home was tastefully, if not a bit sparsely, decorated.

"About a year," he informed her. "I bought it after I sold my condo."

"You lived in a condo?" she asked, brows furrowed in a frown.

"Yeah, why?"

"I don't know. You just always loved wide open spaces. I can't see you cooped up in a condo."

He grinned. "Turns out you're right about that. I couldn't stand it. I bought this place because it felt like a compromise. I have a couple acres—just enough to give me a feeling of space, but not too much to keep me too busy with tending the land."

"You must do an awful lot of mowing," she observed, remembering the expansive, crisp lawn in front of and beside the house.

"I have a riding mower. Besides, I leave most of the property out back in its natural state. When I need to do some thinking, I can amble out there and find privacy among the trees."

"I'm surprised you're not living in the family home," she said, thinking of the stately Victorian the James family had occupied for generations. "Wasn't that the original plan?"

He weighed her words with a wince and a shrug. "I think Dad intended to leave the place to me, but since he's getting older and was apparently holding on to it for the sole purpose of willing it to me, I urged him to sell it. It's just too big, and I don't see myself having a dozen kids to fill all the rooms."

"It was a beautiful home," she mused.

"Beautiful and a bear to heat," he said. "Besides, sometimes sentimentality gets in the way of good sense."

She shot a suspicious glance at him. Was that remark directed at her? Probably not, she decided. It was more likely he believed she was sorely lacking in sentimentality.

"By the way, Dad says hi," he said, interrupting her thoughts. "He's been real worried about you."

She had wondered about Robert. She had expected he would stop by the hospital to see her. "How is your dad?"

"Sick with a bad flu, which is why he stayed away from you the last several days. He was hit with it late Tuesday, after . . ."

After Rennie had passed, she realized. The thought of her grandmother caused a stab of regret to slice through her heart. Why hadn't she made the move to Westover sooner?

"Dad plans to come over the minute Doc gives him the all clear," Mason said. "He's hoping it'll be tomorrow."

"It'll be nice to see him," she said softly.

She couldn't deny she missed Robert, who had been the only real father figure in her life. She knew she should have kept in better touch with him, but the demands of her career had always provided a ready excuse for her to put Westover and its people firmly behind her. It had been a coping mechanism that had served her well. The truth was, Robert was a living, breathing reminder of Westover—and the past she had wanted to erase. A past shrouded in painful mystery.

Years before, her mother, Jessie, had come home after an extended absence, with Lacey in tow. Rennie hadn't known she had a granddaughter until that day. For reasons known only to Jessie, she had left in a hurry that evening, leaving Lacey behind. Later, they had learned Jessie had been killed in a car accident that very night. Surely, Lacey thought, the toddler she'd been understood something was amiss when her mother had never returned.

And what about her father? She had never known anything about him. Perhaps that's why, as a child, she had been so drawn to Robert, climbing into his lap and throwing her arms around his neck at every turn.

Had she even known her father during her very early formative years? she often wondered. She just didn't know the answer to that question, though she longed for it. Regardless, Robert had been patiently tolerant of the little girl who had so craved his affection.

Mason rolled Lacey into what turned out to be a large family room just off a well-appointed kitchen, replete with granite countertops and stainless steel appliances.

"You have a beautiful home," she said. "And I appreciate your letting me stay here."

He waved off her gratitude. "Really, it's not a problem. I'd like to think you'd do the same for me."

When she didn't immediately speak up, he cringed, mock-dramatically. "You'd have left me in the hospital, broken and battered, and homeless. Lacey Jane, that hurts." He touched his heart. "Right here."

"I'm not homeless," she grumbled. "And I'm convinced I

would do just fine on my own. Really, I hate to inconvenience you like this."

"You'd do fine on your own? Great," he said. "Prove it." He dropped onto a nearby leather couch, extending his legs out in front of him—the picture of an entirely relaxed male. "Grab me a soda, will you?"

She bit back a chuckle. "Get it yourself."

She remained silent for a moment, processing. Surely she could get along just fine on her own. People broke bones all the time. "They say necessity is the mother of invention," she mused aloud. "I'm sure, if forced to, I could find a way to manage on my own. I know I could!"

"Lacey, Lacey, Lacey," he intoned. "So, so, so stubborn. Surrender, Lacey Jane. Give your body time to heal. I have the space and you need a place."

She opened her mouth to argue, but he silenced her when he rose and moved to the back of her wheelchair. He rolled her close to a large, plump recliner. He bent to lift the leg rest and then, to her surprise, gently lifted her out of the wheelchair. She felt herself pressed against his rock-hard chest and she gasped at the close contact. When he lowered her into the heavenly comfort of the chair, it took several seconds for her heart to resume its normal rhythm. Weird, she thought.

She didn't have time to contemplate her body's odd reaction to Mason—the nearest thing to a cousin she'd ever had—because he spoke. "All right?" he asked. He towered above her, hands on his hips. "Anything you need? Food? Drink? Reading material?"

Her battered body yearned for rest, and to her surprise, she found her eyelids growing heavy. "This has to be the most comfortable chair I've ever sat in," she said sleepily.

"It oughta be," he said. "It's mine."

* * *

Lacey woke several hours later. Mason was sprawled on the couch, watching a sports program on low volume. "Hey, you're up," he said, swinging his legs onto the floor. He quickly checked his watch. "And it's time for your pain medication."

He hurriedly retrieved the pill from the bottle he'd previously left on the kitchen island. He ducked into the fridge for a bottle of water and opened the top before passing it to her. "There you go," he said.

After she had swallowed the pill, he checked the time again—this time consulting a large clock in the eating nook off the kitchen. "Hey, it's dinnertime. You have to be starving."

"You want me to fix something?" she asked.

He laughed. "Sure thing. I'll just get back to my television program." He made as if to return to the couch, but then turned with a grin and strode to the kitchen island, moving to stand on the side closest to the kitchen appliances. He opened a drawer and pulled out a paper. "Takeout," he said triumphantly. "What sounds good to you? We have it all."

"Pizza sounds good," she told him. "If you can get my purse for me, I'll be happy to pay. By the way," she added, "I fully intend to pay you for allowing me to stay here."

"Are you *kidding?*" he asked. He studied her features and realized she was dead serious. "You are the most stubborn, prideful, ridiculous woman I've ever known. But I guess that's why I—"

"I am none of those things," she cut in. "I am independent, hardworking, and definitely plan *not* to take advantage of your hospitality."

"Why not?" he demanded, incredulous. His narrowed eyes regarded her as if she was a germ under a microscope. "I've known you since you came to this town when you were barely out of diapers. Why is it hard for you to lean on me a little bit?" He appeared to consider his own question as he raked his hand through his hair. "It was always hard for you to lean on me or anyone. Even when you were a kid—"

"A little bit?" she cried. "I'd say your inviting me into your home and acting as my nursemaid constitutes more than me leaning on you a *little* bit." She grew abruptly quiet, but soon roused herself. "Mason, you have a job!"

"I've taken a couple weeks off."

"You have not!" she said, aghast.

He simply nodded. "I have."

"Why would you do that? You're sacrificing your vacation time for me?" She shook her head vigorously. "Take me to Grandma's right now."

He rounded the kitchen island and moved to stand in front of her. He towered over her—a mountain of masculinity. With folded arms, he regarded her with a rueful look on his handsome face. "I'm not taking you anywhere."

"I'm not kidding. Please. Take me to my grandmother's house. I'll be just fine." She attempted to move from the chair, finding the cumbersome cast as immobile as he appeared to be.

He watched her speculatively, taking in the stark look of apprehension in her blue eyes. Or was it terror he saw in the ice blue depths? The sparkle of humor in his eyes vanished. "Lacey, it's all right. Really. You'll be just fine here."

She shook her head vigorously. "Mason, I can't be out of commission like this. I have too much to do." She let out an agonized moan, her eyes widening with a shock of sudden awareness. "I have to plan Grandma's funeral!"

He pulled up a chair and sat down, leaning toward her. "Rennie's church family has taken care of everything. Rennie talked to Dad some time ago about her wishes regarding a funeral service. . . ."

"What were her wishes?" Lacey practically shrieked. "Why didn't she tell *me?*" Suddenly, she felt sick and overwhelmed.

To her mind, her failure to talk to her grandmother about such an important issue was inexcusable—akin to neglect on her part. What kind of granddaughter was she, anyway? In her haste to put her life in Westover behind her, she had effectively banished Rennie from her life.

Sure, she'd called her three times a week—and they had often e-mailed after she'd managed to persuade Rennie to allow her to buy her a computer—but it hadn't been enough. Oh, she was a horrible granddaughter. She felt the tears spring into her eyes, and they spilled onto her cheeks.

"Ah, Lacey," Mason said with a sigh, "everything is going to be fine. The service is already planned for Saturday, and it's everything Rennie wanted. I promise."

She sniffled. "I should have been the one planning the service."

"Honey, you're not in any shape to plan anything."

"I know!" she cried indignantly. "And I'm furious about that!"

He stifled a chuckle. She had never been one to sit still. He knew full well that her confinement in a wheelchair was going to practically kill the girl who had always flitted around, moving from one task to the next. In his mind's eye, he suddenly saw her as a young girl—an overachiever, intent on showing him up at every turn.

Although there were nearly three years between them, she had moved up a grade while in grammar school, and that, coupled with the fact that she was the youngest child in her actual class to begin with, meant that she was only a year behind him in school, when she should have been two years behind.

The age difference hadn't affected her academically, since she shined in her class—often outperforming Mason, who had graduated valedictorian of his senior class. Had she been a senior, rather than a junior, she would have been on the stage delivering the commencement speech, rather than him.

Of course, he'd soon learned that she had quietly managed to accumulate enough credits to graduate early, so she did actually graduate along with his class. Had she pressed the issue, she could have acted as valedictorian. Why hadn't she? He'd always wondered about that.

He and Lacey had been competitive, all right—too competitive. Theirs had been a contentious relationship, although he couldn't deny he'd enjoyed her spirited personality.

"I can't be stuck in this cast," she exclaimed. The thing felt too tight, claustrophobic, and uncomfortable, and if she could have managed it, she would have pried it off her leg with her bare hands. "I have to get out of this thing!"

When he took both her hands between his, she struggled to pull away. He held firm and spoke soothingly. "You don't have a choice. You know it and I know it. Just concentrate on getting well, and stop fighting everything in the process." He released her hands. "Lacey Jane, for once, can you please take the path of least resistance?"

She shook her head. "This isn't part of the plan," she moaned.

"What plan?" he asked with interest.

She swiped at the tears that were once again forming in her eyes. "The plan where I come home and do for my grandmother in her golden years what she did for me, and . . ."

"What?" he prompted. "Tell me."

"The plan where I find my father."

Chapter Four

The next day, Robert strode into his son's home, whistling a tune. He hadn't bothered knocking or ringing the doorbell, and Mason gave him a rueful glance from his place at the kitchen table.

"Where's our girl?" he demanded in his robust voice.

Mason rose and angled a glance at the recliner, simultaneously holding a finger to his lips. "Shhh, she's sleeping, Dad."

"Oh, sorry," he whispered as he tiptoed around for a peek at her.

Lacey was lying back in the recliner, sleeping soundly. Mason knew she'd had a rough night, and he was determined that she get as much rest as possible. She seemed to prefer the recliner to the bed in the downstairs master bedroom.

Robert frowned as he studied her face. "She looks thin—and pale."

Mason expelled a long sigh. "I think she's in more pain than she's letting on. She's devastated about Rennie and blaming herself."

"For what?"

"For arriving too late to say good-bye. For not making the move back home sooner. You know how she is."

"Don't I know it? Always had the weight of the world on her shoulders."

"How are *you* feeling, Pop?" he asked, taking stock of his father's still pale face.

27

"Got the all-clear from Doc," he said cheerily. "I'll tell you what, that was one miserable flu."

"I'll take your word for it," Mason said, making a mock-frightened face, and then taking several steps away from his father.

Robert laughed, and then grimaced when Lacey stirred. He took another look at her and saw she was waking up.

Suddenly, her eyes popped open. She glanced around, disoriented, and then seemed to register where she was. She saw Robert standing over her.

"Hey," she said. "How are you feeling?"

"Better than you," he told her, his eyes passing over her haggard face. "You don't look so good, Lacey Jane."

"Thanks, Pop," she said ruefully.

"I don't mean you don't look beautiful," he said with an impatient sigh. "Just tired and a little beat up."

"I am tired and a little beat up. You look a little pale yourself."

He crossed the room and took a seat on the couch at the far end of the room. Apparently he wasn't taking any chances with his germs. Mason sat closer to her, in the nearby loveseat.

Robert made eye contact with her. "So, Mason told you that Rennie's funeral is planned for Saturday." He raised a hand to clarify. "Actually, she didn't want a funeral, per se. As you know, she wanted to be cremated." He paused to register her reaction. When she remained silent, he continued. "She wants her ashes spread up on Hood Peak, beside Halsey Pond." He smiled softly. "She always said that was her favorite place on earth."

"What's taking place Saturday, then?" Lacey asked, attempting to keep her voice steady. If her voice broke, she knew she would lose it altogether and start bawling.

"A party," he said succinctly. "A party commemorating Rennie's life." He smiled broadly. "She wanted a celebration. She wanted people to gather together and enjoy good food and fellowship."

Lacey sat quietly. So Rennie wanted a party? She realized how different she was from her grandmother, who had a vast collection of friends. Rennie had always enjoyed a rousing get-together, while Lacey preferred the solitude of her own company. She was simply uncomfortable in crowds.

"How . . . do you feel about a party?" Robert asked, watching her speculatively.

"I think that, if it's what Grandma wanted, I have to honor her wishes."

What else could she say? She couldn't very well go against Rennie's final wishes, although she really would have preferred a quiet service with a few close friends.

He nodded. "Good then."

She shifted in the chair, attempting to find a more comfortable position, and when she couldn't manage it, shot the broken leg a dirty look.

He noticed. "That brings me to our next topic of conversation," he said, moving to the edge of the couch and lacing his fingers together. "Lacey, you're going to need more care than Mason is able to give you, so I've hired a nurse to come in and help take care of you for part of each day."

She groaned. "Pop, you don't have to do that. I don't need any help."

He glanced at Mason and shook his head wearily. "Always so proud," he muttered, and then fixed his gaze on her again. "Look, Lacey Jane, like it or not, you're incapacitated, and the fact of the matter is, there are things you're going to need help doing for the next month or two. Things Mason can't really help you with."

"Lord, do we have to have this conversation?" she moaned. She raised both hands, pressing them to her head in frustration.

"Okay, enough said." Robert turned to his son. "Can you manage the rest of the day? The nurse will start tomorrow."

He nodded.

Robert turned his attention back to her. "So, Mason tells me you have something on your mind."

She looked perplexed for a second or two and then remembered her declaration to Mason the day before. She'd told him about her intent to locate her father. Maybe she shouldn't have blurted it out like she had. Maybe she should have kept her intentions to herself for a while. But she had told him and she couldn't take back her words now.

She nodded. "Yes. I'd like to find my father. My biological father," she clarified.

Although Robert was no relation, and she had never resided in his home, she did consider him like a father. In fact, when Lacey was small, Rennie had drawn up her will listing Robert and his now-deceased wife as Lacey's guardians in the event something should happen to her. They had readily agreed to accept the responsibility of raising her if the need arose, just as years before, Rennie had agreed to raise Robert and his brother if something had happened to his parents.

"Have you already started your search?" he inquired.

She nodded. "I've just begun," she said, smoothing a hand across her hair. "I just don't have anything to go on, really." She pinned him with a gaze. "Do you know anything about my father?"

He sighed loudly and shook his head. "I don't know anything. If I did, I'd tell you."

"But you can speculate," she said in an accusing tone. "Lord knows, everyone in this town speculated. . . ."

"Whoa there, young lady," he said. "I know you've spent the last twenty-five years with a chip on your shoulder, blaming everyone in this town for God knows what, but . . ." He raised a finger. "You know I'd tell you if I knew something."

She sighed. "I'm sorry, Pop. I just . . . I just want answers."

"I know you're searching, honey. You've always been searching for something. And I'll do anything I can to help you. But I don't know where to begin. It's the God's honest truth."

He paused and searched her face. "One thing I do know. Your mama was a good woman. I know you heard rumors growing up, and I can promise you this—they weren't true. You mark my words, there's a logical explanation for everything that happened that day she came back to town."

She felt tears welling in her eyes again. Oh, why was she so emotional? Usually, she could keep a rein on her emotions, despite the circumstances in her life.

"I just wish . . ."

"What?" he prompted.

"I just wish I knew why she left me."

He spoke with certainty. "I don't think she planned to leave you. Had the accident not happened, I firmly believe she intended to come back. I don't doubt that for a moment. And I don't doubt that that girl loved you with everything in her. She was a good kid—a lot like you. Smart, determined, kindhearted."

She digested his words and after a long moment said, "Will you help me?"

When he nodded, she turned to Mason. "Will you help me? As sheriff of this town, it seems to me you should be able to help me."

"I'll do what I can," he told her.

"Sometimes I wonder if Rennie knew more than she let on, and just didn't want to tell me," she said.

"Why would she do that?" Robert said. "It doesn't make sense that she would hide anything from you."

She shrugged. "Who knows? As far as I know, Grandma didn't keep any secrets from me. And I had asked her outright if she knew who my father was. She swore to me that she didn't."

She paused, remembering the conversation as if it were yesterday. Rennie had been adamant that she didn't know her father's name, but said if she did, she would personally hunt him down for answers as to why her daughter had left the house that rainy night all those years ago. Had she not gone out that night, she wouldn't have been killed in a car accident just across the state line. Lacey would never forget the steely glint in Rennie's eyes or the firm set of her jaw. No, if Rennie had known, she would have told her.

"If only your mother hadn't left that night," Robert said. "To this day, we wonder why she didn't leave a note behind. Jessie had always been so responsible."

Lacey shrugged again. "Maybe she changed. Grandma said she only came home to visit a few times during her freshman year of college, and then nothing after that, which apparently wasn't like her. And when she finally did show up with me that day, she hadn't called ahead. She just appeared. And unfortunately, Grandma had had to dash out for some reason of her own, so . . ."

"So she wasn't there, and therefore couldn't know what had prompted your mother to take off like she did—and so soon after arriving," Mason said.

"Wait, I remember," Lacey blurted, feeling as if her brain wasn't functioning properly and she was slow on the uptake. "One of Rennie's friend's daughters was having a baby, and there were complications. Her friend called, begging Grandma to come. She hated to leave, of course, but apparently my mother assured her they would have a long talk when she got back and get everything sorted out."

"Why did Rennie take you along with her that day?" Mason wondered aloud.

"I remember," Robert said. "Apparently, Jessie hadn't slept much for days. She was exhausted and wasn't feeling well. Rennie insisted she go to bed while she watched Lacey. Anyway, when Rennie got the call from her friend, she took Lacey with her, rather than wake Jessie. Frankly, she was eager to show her off. To that day, she hadn't known she had a granddaughter. She was thrilled." He sighed. "Well, thank God Rennie did take you with her that day, because if you'd been in the car with your mother . . ."

"I probably would have been killed too," Lacey murmured, and then sat quietly for a long moment before she spoke again. "Grandma always figured that my mother received a call from my father that day, prompting her to leave." She shrugged. "But who knows? Maybe it wasn't even him. But if it was, what did he say that made her leave Westover like that?"

"And why did your mother apparently leave him and come back to town in the first place?" Robert mused.

"Maybe they had fought," she speculated. "Or maybe she didn't leave him at all." She shrugged. "We're assuming there was a man in the picture at that point. Maybe he was long gone. Maybe my mother simply thought it was time to visit her mother. If only Grandma and my mom had found the time to really talk that day she came home."

Robert nodded, a contemplative look on his face.

"Your mother dropped out of college, didn't she?" Mason said.

Lacey shrugged. "My understanding is she dropped out early, but who knows when specifically. Again, if only she and Rennie had had time to talk. I know Grandma used to just about make herself sick thinking about that missed opportunity, wishing with all her heart her friend hadn't called her that day. It was difficult for her."

"So all we really know is that your mother showed up at home with you in tow, and we have no idea why," Robert said. "Hence, all the town gossip about her."

Chapter Five

As Lacey struggled to get ready for bed that evening, she resolved never to take her mobility for granted again. It had been mortifying when Mason had rolled her into the bathroom and then closed his eyes as he attempted to help her undress. She had finally shooed him out, promising to call him if she needed him.

Finally, in frustration, she had washed her face, brushed her teeth, and then opted to remain dressed in the clothes she was wearing. With a good deal of effort, she had managed to use the toilet and then hoist herself back into the wheelchair. She had jostled the leg some, but decided not to mention it to Mason.

He was terribly protective, and she railed against it, just as she had done when they were kids. Unfortunately, when she attempted to roll herself out of the bathroom, she found she just didn't have the upper body strength to manage it. Weakened by the accident, she felt both light-headed and fatigued.

He knocked on the door. "Are you okay in there? Need a hand?"

She struggled to back up the wheelchair so he could open the door.

"Come in," she called in a dispirited voice.

"You're still in your clothes," he observed.

"And I'm going to stay that way. Could you push me out of here?"

He entered the bathroom and obligingly pushed her out of the room. "You look exhausted."

"I am," she said with a yawn.

"So you're ready for bed then?"

She nodded and he detoured toward the large bed. She looked around. She hadn't paid much attention to the room before, but noted it was most definitely a man's room. The bedroom suite was constructed of dark, polished wood. The bed was king size, and covered with a dark, patterned comforter. There was one painting on the wall, featuring an outdoor scene.

"What do you think of the room?" he asked.

She shrugged. "It's you."

"What does that mean?" he asked, curious.

"It means it reminds me of you—kind of dark, sparse . . ." She shrugged, searching for words.

"Are you suggesting I'm vacant and lacking personality?" he inquired, eyeing her with humor.

She chuckled. "I didn't say it, you did."

"Ah, you love me, and you know it. Hey, so you know, I haven't finished decorating the place. I've been . . . busy."

"Busy with what?"

"Work, for one thing," he told her. "But I have grand plans for this room."

"Uh-huh," she muttered, eyeing the bed. She longed to stretch out in it, and the sooner he left, the sooner she could relax.

"Aren't you going to ask me what my plans are?"

"No."

He chuckled. "You are, without a doubt, the most contrary woman I have ever met."

"Me, contrary? Ha! What about you?"

"You think I'm contrary?"

"History has shown you to be," she said with conviction. "Contrary and egotistical."

He appeared taken aback. "You think I'm egotistical too?" A mock-wounded expression flitted across his face.

"Well, you used to be," she said with a yawn.

"Give me an example," he demanded. "I want one example of my supposed arrogance."

"Okay, fine." She racked her brain and then roused herself. "Okay, here's one. Remember the time, in front of all your buddies, you told me to wear your number at a football game?"

He appeared to search his memory, stroking his chin thoughtfully. "Okay, yeah, I remember that. I wasn't being egotistical."

"Yes, you were."

"No, I wasn't. And I didn't *tell* you, I *asked* you."

"So why did you expect me to wear your number at the football game if you weren't being egotistical?"

He eyed her speculatively. "Oh, I don't know. Maybe if you think on it hard enough, you might figure out why a young guy would ask a pretty girl to wear his number at a football game."

"Oh, Mason, you asked all the girls to wear your number at the games," she reminded him.

"I did not."

She yawned. "Oh, it doesn't matter."

"Maybe it does," he said. "Maybe I asked you because—"

She raised her hand to silence him. "This is silly." She yawned again. "I'm tired. . . ."

Her words dwindled as he bent to lift her out of the wheelchair. He didn't immediately put her down on the bed, but instead gently sat on the edge of the bed with her still in his arms, careful not to jostle her. He grinned into her upturned face.

"What are you doing?" she demanded in a shrill voice.

"You seem to be rewriting history, Lacey Jane," he said. "And I'm going to set you straight. If you'll remember, Jake Colton asked you to wear his number to the football game, and you did. And if you'll recall, his very angry girlfriend, whom you didn't know existed, marched up to you—with her friends in tow—and demanded to know why you were wearing his number."

Suddenly she remembered. He was right. She had been humiliated. Although she was certain Mason hadn't witnessed the event, apparently he'd heard about it. He had shown up moments later with *his* friends in tow, and had suggested she wear his number instead. It had been a second humiliation, adding insult to injury.

"I remember!" she cried indignantly. "You were intent on embarrassing me, after that jerk—what's his name—had already embarrassed me."

"Lacey, if you weren't already battered and broken, I'd be tempted to drop you on this bed," he muttered. "I didn't try to embarrass you that night. I tried to . . ."

"I don't want to talk about it," she interrupted, fighting back the tears. Lord, why the heightened emotionalism? She was a grown woman. But then, she knew why she felt so fragile and upset. Rennie was dead. Her beloved grandmother had passed away. And Mason was practically holding her prisoner in his house, and now in his arms.

She sniffled and fought the tears threatening to spill. "Will you put me down, please? My leg is killing me."

He rose and gingerly laid her on the bed. "One day, you're going to let me finish a complete thought. Have you noticed how . . . ?"

Her head tipped to the side on the pillow, and she was out like a light. He stared at her face, taking in the blond lashes fanning out over her high cheekbones. He gently smoothed the hair from her brow and bent to kiss her good night. Once again, she had prevented him from saying his piece. But then, what else was new?

* * *

Lacey woke the next morning to sunlight streaming in through the gaps in the very masculine curtains. She blinked against the light, until it was abruptly blocked by a stout, matronly figure standing beside her bed. She squinted to see who was there. She broke into a wide smile when she recognized the older nurse from the hospital who had washed her hair and then later had regaled her with stories to keep her spirits up.

"Hello," she said, attempting to sit up.

"No, no, don't rise so abruptly," the woman said. "Take it slow and easy." She helped her up by gently grasping her arm and assisting her into a sitting position.

"Thanks."

Mason walked into the room, smiling widely. "I see you've met Millie. You may remember her from the hospital."

She nodded. "I do. It's great to see you again."

"And it's great to see you with a little color in your cheeks," Millie said.

"It turns out we caught Millie just as she was finishing up her final week at the hospital," he informed Lacey. "Fortunately for us, she's agreed to continue working for me until you're on the mend."

Lacey frowned, doing a mental calculation of the cost of hiring a full-time nurse. Could she afford it?

He noticed the look on her face, and understood immediately that the wheels were turning in her proud head. "Lacey . . . ," he said with chagrin, and then turned to Millie. "Anything I can do to help out this morning?"

"You can help me get her into the bathroom," she said briskly. "I'm sure she's longing for a refreshing shower."

"I am," she said, but cast a hesitant glance at Mason. "I think we can manage it without his help."

"Why would you want *my* help?" he muttered.

"Oh, we do want your help, Sheriff," Millie assured him.

"We really don't want to jostle that leg. After a few more days, we won't have to baby it so much, but for now . . ."

Lacey shot a glance at the leg. She hadn't really studied the contraption that encircled it. Her eyes widened. It wasn't a cast in the real sense of the word. It was the stuff of science fiction!

The leg was encased in a black splint of some type, with stainless steel rods running from the top of her thigh down to her foot, both along the inside and outside of her leg. A row of metal pins protruded from the interior sides of the splint and disappeared into her leg. She suddenly felt woozy and gulped.

"Try not to look at it," Millie cautioned. "It looks scarier than it is, but those pins will work wonders toward healing the leg. Modern medicine," she said softly. "Thank the Lord for modern medicine."

Lacey took a deep breath and cast a glance at Mason. He nodded encouragingly and then strode to the bed and carefully scooped her into his arms.

After gently depositing her in the wheelchair, he left the room so Millie could wheel her into the bathroom and help her with her morning routine.

Once done, they joined him in the kitchen, where he was preparing a breakfast of bacon and eggs. "Will you join us, Millie?" he asked. "There's plenty."

"Thanks, hon, but no thanks. I've already eaten." She glanced at Lacey and arched a brow. "He cooks. I'm impressed."

"Yep, I make a mean egg," he said gamely.

"Well, I'd be happy to take over the cooking and light housekeeping," Millie offered. "It'll give me something to do. I can't just sit around waiting for Lacey to decide she needs my help."

He nodded. "You'd probably be doing a lot of waiting," he agreed.

"Oh, for Pete's sake," she said. "I know when I need help."

"Glad to hear it," he said with a grin. "Need any help with anything?"

"No!"

"Well, I'm off to tidy up the bedroom," Millie declared.

"You don't have to," Mason and Lacey said in unison.

"I have to earn my keep," she said cheerfully. "I don't want you and your father thinking you're not getting your money's worth." She was off then, hurrying to the bedroom and humming a cheery tune.

"I think we hit the jackpot there," Mason said.

"I think you're right," she concurred. "Oh, and I will pay you back."

He chose not to respond, certain if he did, she would get worked up, and he didn't want her worked up. He wanted her relaxed and comfortable. "Eat your breakfast," he said.

After breakfast, he sought her eyes from across the table. "I've been thinking," he began.

"About what?"

He was silent for a moment, apparently processing, but finally spoke. "You mentioned yesterday that your mom left college early. . . ."

"That's right," she said. "I think she told Grandma that much."

"And she didn't come directly home," he remembered.

"Right again. And we have no idea where she went, but that wherever she went, she gave birth to me while she was there."

"Dad tells me your mom and grandma were always so close. I wonder why Jessie didn't confide in Rennie long before she came home."

Lacey shook her head, spreading her hands uncertainly.

"What if . . . ," Mason began.

"What?"

"What if Jessie simply met a man, got married, had a baby, dropped out of school, and . . ."

"Maybe not necessarily in that order. Why wouldn't she have told Grandma if she'd gotten married?" she mused, but then met his gaze. "Because," she said triumphantly, "because Grandma had warned her about marrying young. Grandma had implored her to finish her education before she thought about settling down with a man—just like she begged me to wait until I had some life experience and six years of college and law school under my belt before settling down."

She sat quietly for several seconds, and then glanced up. "She always encouraged me to do well in school. 'Education is the key,' she always said. She talked a lot about losing Grandpa when he was so young, and having to survive without the means to support herself. She said if it hadn't been for your grandmother, who was always there to help, she wouldn't have made it."

Mason nodded his head up and down in measured intervals. "You could be right. Maybe your mom felt as if she'd let Rennie down. And who knows? There may be other circumstances that prevented her from telling Rennie."

"Like maybe she made a huge mistake," she said sadly. "Maybe it was a bad marriage—provided there was a marriage. That would account for her running back home without a husband."

He stroked his jaw. "You know, we really can only speculate. Maybe Jessie didn't run home at all, as in 'run' to escape something or someone. Maybe she simply came for a short visit. By the way, I've been wondering, how do you know there was a phone call? Did anyone try to trace that call?"

"Grandma said she found the phone moved from the countertop beside the refrigerator. That's where she always kept it. When she got home that night, she found it on the table edge, and the receiver was dangling off. She figured it meant my mother had either called someone or had received a call."

She shook her head sadly, but roused herself. "Okay, so if you're right and my mother got married, then is it likely the college would have some record of her name change? If she did get married, let's hope she did it while still attending college."

"It's a good place to start."

"You mean, paying a visit to the college," she said hopefully.

"You're not visiting anywhere anytime soon," he said. When she made a dispirited face, he raised a conciliatory hand. "Look, I'll make a few phone calls. I doubt I can learn much, with all the privacy laws these days, but I'll sure give it the old college try."

"And if you're unsuccessful, we can pay the college a visit?" she asked, her eyes imploring.

"Absolutely."

"And Mason, I need to go home—to Grandma's. I need—"

"I know, Lacey. I know."

Chapter Six

Three days later, Lacey rose early with Millie's help. She had to admit the sweet-tempered nurse was an absolute godsend, tending to her needs kindly and efficiently. Whenever she thought about Rennie and felt tears threatening to spill, Millie seemed to sense her melancholy, and she would disappear for several moments to allow Lacey time to cry, and then she returned and always managed to draw her out of her grief.

Her leg pain wasn't nearly as intense as it had been, although she was careful not to jostle it too much. She still relied on pain pills, which Millie insisted were required at prescribed times so as to stay on top of the pain.

"How's the leg?" Mason asked when he popped his head into the bedroom.

"Better," she told him, and then noticed he was in uniform. "And where are you off to, Sheriff?"

He arched a brow. "Am I to infer from that remark that you care where I'm off to, counselor?"

"Just curious," she told him.

"Thought I'd better check in at the department, to ensure my undersheriff has things under control. I won't be long." He glanced at Millie. "Do you think it would be all right to take her out for a drive today, if we manage to keep the leg propped up?"

Lacey's eyes widened eagerly. "Home?"

He nodded.

Millie weighed the question with a tilt of her head. "If you're careful, it should be all right. We want to keep the leg supported for a few more days, but then we'll gradually allow her to move it around a bit more."

"Will the doctor take this contraption off my leg soon?" she asked.

She shook her head. "'Fraid not, honey, but once the bones are better secured in place and the healing is well under way, you'll be able to lower the leg and rely on crutches once in a while."

"That'll be great," she said wistfully, and then quirked a grin. "Mason's going to end up in a chiropractor's office from lifting me all the time."

"I'm not complaining," he said, and then made a play of rubbing his back as he left the room with a theatrical moan.

"He is so cute," Millie said with a grin. "If I was twenty years younger . . ."

Lacey watched after him. Mason, cute?

Millie chuckled. "You should see the way the ladies of this town fawn all over our sheriff. When he comes into the hospital with a suspect, or to check on an injured deputy or citizen, the women just go weak in the knees. Oh, and that smile of his. He can just about melt butter with a look."

Lacey's voice was flat when she spoke. "Mason?"

"Don't tell me you haven't noticed the man is drop-dead gorgeous! You have eyes, girl!" she chided, and then said ruefully, "Maybe you need glasses. Have you had your vision checked lately?"

She laughed. "My eyes are fine. I guess I still see Mason through the same eyes as I did when we were kids. Back then, he reminded me of a . . ."

"What?"

Lacey laughed again, searching her mind for just the right

description of him as a youngster. "Of a . . . big . . . festering blister."

Millie burst out laughing. "That's just plain disgusting. That man is no festering blister." She chuckled heartily, and then sobered. "At least I hope not." She grimaced. "Oh, my, I may never look at him the same again."

"I apologize for the imagery," Lacey said with a sigh. "And I guess if I'm being honest with myself . . ."

"He's no longer a festering blister?"

She shook her head. "No, I guess not. He is pretty easy on the eyes, huh?"

"I'll say. You grew up together, didn't you?"

She nodded. "My grandma Rennie and his grandma Peggy were best friends since childhood. When my grandpa died when Rennie was still a young woman and she was left with a young daughter to take care of, Peggy and her husband, Ben, made sure she was okay." She was silent, thinking. "It's funny. Peggy was born to a very wealthy family. . . ."

"The Moores," Millie said. "And of course, Ben also came from a wealthy family."

"Right. And Grandma came from the poorest family in town, yet she and Peggy were as close as sisters." She laughed. "As the story goes, they met in kindergarten. They attended the one-room schoolhouse out by Halsey Pond. I guess the first day of school, some boy tugged on Peggy's pigtail and made her cry. Grandma Rennie saw him do it, and she took off after him. She apparently pummeled the little guy."

Millie chuckled. "Poor little fellow."

"Oh, *Ben* recovered soon enough," she relayed with a chuckle. "He always said he fell for Peggy that very day. He said he couldn't help himself and had to touch that pigtail."

"So he's the same Ben that Peggy married!"

She nodded. "Yep. And Grandma married Leonard Karr."

"You never knew your grandfather, did you?" Millie said, and shook her head. "No, no, he passed long before you came along."

"You're right, I never met him. I understand he was a wonderful man. A big man, gentle as a lamb, Grandma always said."

"That's right," Millie said, smiling softly. "I met him years ago. He was actually a close friend of my father's."

Lacey's jaw dropped open. "Small town," she mused, and then perked up. "Did you know my mother, Jessie Karr?"

Millie nodded her head slowly, a smile flitting across her face. "Jessie and I were great friends through our school years."

"So you went to high school together?" Lacey asked, her eyes wide in anticipation of her answer.

"No, I started high school here, but ended up finishing in Morton, a couple hours north of here. I moved back here after I got married."

Lacey was silent for a moment. "Are you . . . Have you heard . . . ?"

"All the rumors and speculation about your mother?" she asked sternly. "Yes, and I never believed a word of it. Jessie was the most down-to-earth, kind-hearted, and intelligent girl I knew. I know when she ran off that night and was killed in the car wreck, many, many people had a lot to say about it. But Lacey, hear me, and hear me good—your mama was a good person. She would have no more run off and left you than hack off her own head. There's more to the story of that night. You mark my words."

"People change," Lacey said softly. "Maybe . . . she changed."

Millie shook her head adamantly. "She did not. I refuse to believe that."

She smiled tremulously. "Can I tell you something, Millie?"

The woman nodded, her eyes clear and sincere.

"I want to find my father. I want to know who he is. I want to know if it was him who called my mother that night she was killed." She sighed loudly. "I need to know what happened all those years ago."

Millie grasped her hand and gave it a squeeze. "Of course you do. You're human. And you have a right to know."

She sighed. "I often wonder if my father is alive, and if so, did he know about me?"

"Of course he knew," she said with certainty. "Jessie would never . . ." Suddenly she frowned. "Well . . . if Jessie kept you a secret from him, she had good reason."

"But suppose he did know about me. If so, why didn't he come for me?" she wondered aloud. "What kind of a man abandons a child?"

Millie shook her head. "Unfortunately, too many men do that very thing."

"Deadbeat dads. I've dealt with my share in my line of work."

"That's right!" Millie said gleefully. "You're an attorney." She leaned closer to Lacey, her eyes alight with excitement. "Do you think you'll open your own law office in Westover? Lord knows we need a good attorney here."

She smiled and considered the question. She really hadn't given the idea serious consideration, although it had occurred to her. The reality was, if she'd ultimately settled in Westover to care for Rennie, it only made sense she would have needed to secure employment. But the cost of opening her own office . . .

Thinking about her line of work caused her thoughts to drift to Keith, one of the founding partners of the firm she had worked at in Portland. She'd been at the law office for five years, and at the age of almost twenty-nine, was one of the most successful attorneys at the large downtown firm. Upon her hire there, Keith had dangled the carrot of a possible partnership, but it had never come to fruition. Each time Lacey had broached the subject, Keith had put her off, promising good things to come. When he had recently suggested a different kind of partnership with her, she had rejected his overtures and realized it was time to move on. That reality was part of her willingness to pack up and leave Portland for Westover. It wasn't as if her career had been moving in the direction she'd hoped.

She sighed. Keith had been persistent, however, and upon realizing she truly intended to leave the firm, he had once again made promises about making her a partner. He'd even given her a date as to when the announcement would take place. However, with Rennie's illness, and his propensity for deception, she had opted to make the move anyway.

When the telephone on the bedside table rang, both she and Millie nearly jumped out of their skins.

"Oh my," Millie said. "That startled me." She reached for the phone. "James residence. Yes, hold on please." She capped the phone with her hand and whispered, "It's a Keith Dunne on the line."

Speak of the devil, Lacey thought. Keith's timing had always been impeccable, except when it came to granting her a partnership. "Thanks, Millie," she mouthed, and accepted the receiver. "Keith," she said smoothly.

His concerned voice exploded in her ear. "Lacey, I heard the news! How are you?"

"I'm a little worse for wear," she said, and then frowned. "How'd you hear?"

"I called the number you left for your grandmother's, and when no one answered and you didn't return my messages, I got worried. I ended up calling the sheriff's office and was finally apprised of what had happened to you and where you were."

"Did you call today?" she wondered aloud. If so, Mason

had likely been aware of the call. The thought gave her pause, and for the life of her, she couldn't imagine why.

"Yeah, today. Oh, and Lacey, I'm so sorry about your grandmother."

"Thank you, Keith."

"Uh, at the risk of seeming uncouth, I do have to ask. Does this change anything as to your future plans? With your grandmother gone, you don't have any reason to stay in Westover, do you?"

Did she? Was there anything, other than a badly broken leg, keeping her from hitting the road?

Yes. She needed answers about her father and mother.

"I'm in no condition to travel, and won't be for some time," she told him. "So I'll be here for a while."

"Well, so you know, I'm sorry for putting off the decision about making you a partner in the firm. It's waiting for you when you come back. And Lacey, I do hope you come back."

"I'll give it a lot of thought," she assured him.

"I'll keep in touch then. Can I reach you at this number?"

"For the foreseeable future," she told him.

"Take care."

"Will do."

She passed the phone to Millie, who returned it to the hook. "Well, he sounded like a nice young man."

Lacey smiled. Could you tell "nice" in a voice? She wasn't so certain exactly how nice Keith was. But all the same, she wouldn't burn her bridges just yet. She'd worked long and hard for that partnership, and it seemed it was now hers for the taking.

Chapter Seven

Mason gingerly loaded Lacey into the cab of his pickup truck and then hurried around to climb in. He assessed their sitting arrangements with a critical glance. Since she was petite, she was able to sit fairly comfortably with her back pressed against the door and her leg outstretched on the seat. Belting in proved rather ungainly, however, and she gave up trying.

Mason studied the seatbelt situation and then strapped her in as best he could from the driver's side. "I'll just have to drive extra carefully, so as not to hit any bumps," he said.

The diesel truck roared to life. He shifted into drive, but paused briefly and cast Lacey another appraising glance. "I wonder if we should have put you beside me, with your leg toward the door."

"I'm fine," she assured him.

"Hmm," he murmured. "I don't think so."

He turned off the truck and climbed out, rounding the front to open the passenger-side door. "Here, turn around." He helped her turn, careful that her leg didn't drop off the seat. Satisfied that she was more secure, he closed the door and climbed back into the truck.

He belted her in, and to her dismay, she found herself pressed against him as he drove. When he draped his arm over her to hold her more securely in the seat, she felt her breath hitch in her throat.

"Uh, you don't have to do that," she said. "I'm sure you need your arm for driving."

He gave her a quizzical glance. "I can drive just fine with one hand. Besides, if I was to hit something, or something hit me, I want to be able to hold you in place."

"Well, that's awfully nice of you," she said, "but I'm sure it's not necessary."

He didn't budge, and she felt the warmth of his arm against her torso as he held her snugly against him. She tipped her face down. Did she remember his arm being so muscular? And did he always have the dusting of golden hair on his tanned skin? And oh, had he always been so strong? His arm felt like a vise, immovable and so beautifully formed it reminded her of a carving.

Good grief. This was Mason! Mason, the closest thing to a cousin she'd ever had. Mason, the festering blister.

She laughed at the imagery—a nervous, tight laugh—and he gave her a questioning glance. "What's so funny?"

"I was just remembering what a pain in my butt you used to be," she told him.

He didn't immediately respond. "That's all a matter of perception. By the way, your perceptions were all wrong. Probably still are," he added for good measure.

"So, you weren't a pain in the butt?"

"Sometimes," he admitted, "but you cornered the market on being a pain in the backside."

"I did not!" she said, aghast.

"Heck, Lacey, you were a pain even when you were a tiny tot."

"What's that supposed to mean?" she demanded.

"You were always too smart for your own good," he said. "But"—he raised a finger—"you weren't quite smart enough to keep yourself out of mischief."

"If I found myself in any kind of mischief, it was because I was either following you or running away from you. Besides, isn't that what little kids do? Get into mischief?"

He didn't respond, but she felt his grip on her tighten as he rounded a bend and pulled into the driveway of her grandmother's home. He parked the truck and they sat quietly for a moment, studying the house. The small Victorian, situated on a five-acre parcel just outside of town, stood against a backdrop of scraggly trees.

"It needs paint," Lacey observed sadly, softly. "I'd planned to surprise Grandma by painting it for her this summer."

"Do you think you'll keep the place?" he asked.

She thought for a moment, and then shrugged. "I don't know. I can't bear the thought of parting with it." She turned as best she could in the seat and met his concerned gaze. "I appreciate your bringing me here," she told him. "It's going to be hard to go in, knowing Grandma won't be there to greet me."

He gave her a comforting squeeze. "I know. And you sure don't have to do this today, if you're not ready."

She sat quietly for several long seconds. "I miss her, you know."

He nodded. "Of course you do. I miss her too. And Dad is just plain devastated. She was like a second mom to him."

She nodded, attempting to keep the tears at bay. She couldn't bear the thought of breaking down in front of Mason. Crying was something she rarely did, and she certainly didn't want an audience to her grief. She'd been like that even as a small child.

When she had hurt herself as a kid, she had refused to cry in front of anyone other than her grandmother. Instead, she would bite down on her lower lip until she had her emotions in check. If anyone tried to comfort her or give her sympathy, she would inevitably dart away and seek a private place to cry.

She remembered one time she had taken a tumble off

Robert's front porch. She'd been tiny, maybe three or four. She had landed in a rose bush, and the thorns had pierced her from the top of her head to her feet. Mason had seen her go down and had run for his father, who was home from his office eating lunch.

Robert had gingerly disengaged her from the thorny limbs. He had tried to pull her into a hug, to soothe her, but she had pulled away and took off running. Mason had found her later, hiding behind a tree in the backyard.

"What are you doing?" he had demanded. "Dad is worried about you!"

She had swiped at her runny nose. "Lacey Jane don't need no hugs," she had said.

Oh, it was all right if she was the one doling them out, but if the hug was connected to any form of sympathy directed her way, she flat-out resisted.

Lacey didn't realize she was crying now until she heard her own sobs. When Mason shifted in the seat and wrapped both arms around her, she felt the familiar urge to pull away. But she also found herself experiencing an unfamiliar urge—the urge to surrender to his comfort.

No. She was fine.

She pulled away, and when he spoke, repeating the very words she'd just remembered, she gasped. "Lacey Jane don't need no hugs," he said, and then laughed softly. "Stubborn, stubborn woman."

Inside her grandmother's cozy living room, Lacey resisted the urge to cry again. It was bad enough Mason had seen her weakness before. She wasn't about to let it happen again.

She wanted to move freely around the room, picking up and touching the various mementos that had been so dear to Rennie.

Unfortunately, she could barely get around the tight space in the cumbersome wheelchair.

She sent a quick glance at Mason, who stood just inside the open front door. His sad eyes reflected his own pain, and her heart went out to him.

When he moved to a picture window and stared out onto the once-manicured lawn, she contemplated her next move. If only she could get out of the chair long enough, she could balance herself on the back of the couch and other furniture, in order to visit each of the rooms of the home. She desperately wanted to see Rennie's room upstairs, but knew getting up the tight stairway was an impossibility in a wheelchair. And she certainly wasn't going to ask Mason to carry her upstairs.

Instead, she made her move quickly, setting the wheelchair brake and bracing her hands on the sides of the chair. She hoisted her body up and made a grab for the back of the couch. If Mason hadn't turned at that instant, she might have made a successful escape attempt. Instead, he lunged for her and deposited her back into the chair.

He stood towering over her, hands on hips, wearing an angry expression on his face. "Lacey, are you trying to cripple yourself?" he demanded. "You heard what the doctor said."

"I need to move around," she moaned. "I need to go upstairs and see Grandma's room."

He shook his head. "Not today."

"And I need to get into the attic, to see if I can find anything that might help answer my questions about—"

"*Definitely* not today," he said sharply. "This wasn't a good idea," he said from between clenched teeth. "I should have known better. What was I thinking?"

To her horror, Mason scooped her out of the chair and carried her back to the truck.

"Mason James, you put me down!" she cried. "I need to look around. I need to—"

"You need to go back to my place and sit in my recliner," he said, failing to mask his anger. "You need to listen to me for once in your life."

She heard the click of his keyless remote and she found herself pressed against his chest as he struggled to open the door. Once done, he helped her onto the seat again. He aimed a stern finger at her. "Don't move! I need to lock up."

He strode off, his stiff posture evidence of his frustration. Well, Lacey thought, he wasn't the only one who was frustrated. If he'd left his keys behind, she would have driven off with his truck and left him standing in the front yard.

Well, maybe not, she conceded. Driving with one foot on the pedals and the other lying perpendicular on the front seat . . . It was a logistical impossibility. But soon . . . soon she would be on the mend and out from under Mason's thumb.

Chapter Eight

Later that evening, Lacey and Mason sat in his family room. Once again, he was sprawled out on the couch and she was in the comfortable recliner. He was intently watching a sports program, apparently unconcerned that she was bored to tears. She punctuated her boredom with a yawn, and he glanced over and met her gaze.

"You don't like this program?"

"Nope," she told him. "I've never been much of a football fan."

"Huh," he said, and turned his attention back to the television. He was silent for several moments, but turned to her when a commercial came on.

"By the way," he said in a tone she couldn't quite read, "some guy called the station asking about you."

"Oh?"

"He said he was your boss." He eyed her speculatively then. "I thought you quit that job."

"I did."

"Because of the move?"

"That, and because he made promises he failed to keep," she told him.

"Oh, yeah? Like what?"

She sighed. She wasn't much in the mood to have this conversation. Perhaps if she stalled long enough, the football game would come back on and she wouldn't be obliged to answer his questions.

When the commercials appeared to be unending, and he continued to watch her impatiently, she finally answered him. "Oh, he promised to make me a partner in the firm, but the promotion never materialized."

He nodded. "So you wanted to be a partner, eh? Isn't the firm one of the biggest in Portland?"

She nodded this time. "Yep, and I worked my butt off for that promotion."

"I imagine you did," he said softly. "You always were an overachiever."

"So were you," she said.

"You inspired me," he said with a grin. "Always breathing down my neck—always prodding me along by trying to out-shine me academically."

Lacey attempted to sit more upright in the chair, but her lower extremities wouldn't cooperate and her arms only flailed ineffectively against the sides. Her leg felt like a dead weight, and she finally gave up. "I didn't bust my butt to make you look bad. I worked hard because I had . . ."

"What?" he said, watching her quizzically.

"I had a plan. I had to do well."

"Why?" he asked, his brows furrowed in a frown.

"Because I had something to prove."

"And what's that? That all work and no play make Lacey a dull girl?"

"Thanks," she said drolly.

"Tell me, Lacey, what did you have to prove and to whom did you have to prove it?"

She smiled, though her eyes held no humor. "That I was . . . good enough. And I needed to prove it to . . . everybody."

There, she'd said it. She'd never vocalized it before, to any-one other than herself, but she'd finally admitted to another human being that she had always felt less than in this town.

She'd always felt as if people were judging her for the mistakes of her mother—whatever they might have been.

He sat up on the couch and watched her, his mouth slightly agape. He shook his head. "Everybody . . . meaning me, and Dad, and the occupants of this little berg?" he said, watching her as if she were a space alien.

"Well, yeah," she admitted.

To her surprise, he picked up the television remote and turned off the game. He rose and crossed the room, dropping onto a knee in front of her. His eyes bored into hers. "Lacey, why would you *ever* think you're not good enough?"

She shook her head and shrugged. "I don't want to talk about this. You're going to miss your game." She nodded toward the TV. "You'd better turn it back on."

"Come on, talk to me," he urged.

"Mason, I really don't want to have this conversation," she said, suddenly feeling a headache coming on.

He smiled enigmatically and then rose from his knee. He grasped both sides of the chair, bent, and stared intently into her eyes for a long moment. Finally, his eyes narrowed, and for a fleeting second, she saw something in them—some emotion she couldn't identify. Good lord, was he going to kiss her?

No way. He wouldn't kiss her. He was like a cousin, and he wasn't the least bit attracted to her. And lord knew she wasn't attracted to him. When he pulled back, she breathed a sigh of relief. He only shook his head and walked back to the couch, dropping heavily onto the plush, leather cushions. He continued to watch her, and finally spoke.

"Lacey, so you know, people really aren't standing around talking about you. Most people have enough problems of their own that they don't need to worry about yours. Trust me on that count."

"Well, thanks for clarifying that for me," she said. "I'll keep that in mind the next time I'm at the hardware store or at church, and suddenly everyone stops talking when they see me."

"Wow, you do think a lot of yourself, don't you?" He raked a hand through his hair. "Actually, the truth is, you don't think much of yourself at all, do you?"

She pressed her eyelids shut and found herself counting to ten. She didn't want to have this conversation and for a brief second considered plugging her ears and singing at the top of her lungs. Doggone the leg, she thought, since it assured she was his captive audience.

"You know what I think?" she said in a surly tone. "I think I'm tired of this conversation. I think I'm tired of this broken leg, and I think I'm tired of . . . you!"

Although Mason had scheduled Millie to come help with Lacey's care Monday through Friday, he'd asked if she could come Saturday, early, to help get her ready for Rennie's farewell party.

He knew it would be an emotional day for her, despite how she tried to hide her grief. And after the argument they had had the evening before, he thought it might be nice to have Millie there to serve as a buffer. Why did he always seem to rub her the wrong way? It wasn't his intent—never had been.

He knocked lightly on the door to the downstairs master bedroom and, to his surprise, found Lacey awake and sitting up in bed. "Millie should be here any minute," he told her. "How are you feeling?"

She simply nodded, afraid to speak. She prayed for the strength to get through the upcoming several hours. Oh, why had Rennie wanted a party? She would have so much preferred a quiet service.

However, since she couldn't very well miss the event, she attempted to put on a brave face. She dreaded seeing many people she hadn't seen in years. Westover was just so small that she knew she would likely recognize most of the town's residents who came to commemorate Rennie's life.

Mason stood silently by and watched the emotions crisscross her lovely face. He knew this day would be hard for her and wished he could ease her pain.

"What are you thinking?" he asked finally, drawing her out of her reverie.

"I'm thinking about Grandma."

"And dreading what's to come," he said knowingly.

She nodded. "You know, Grandma and I had so much in common, with one exception. She loved people and crowds—and parties."

"And you don't." He shrugged. "You have different personalities," he said. "Rennie was an extrovert and you're an introvert. It's no big deal. Look at me and Dad. We don't have much in common, but we get along great."

"Mason, you were adopted, remember? That might account for your differing personalities."

"Well, sure." He tipped his head to the side and eyed her thoughtfully. "Lacey, if it all gets to be too much for you, just give me some kind of a signal and I'll get you out of there."

"Do you promise?"

"You know I do," he said. "What's the signal going to be?"

"I could always run screaming from the room," she said. "Wait, no can do." She shot a withering glance at her broken leg.

"How about you whisper in my ear, 'Get me the heck out of here'?"

"That oughta work," she said gratefully.

Chapter Nine

Lacey lasted about two hours at the party, and then the fatigue descended over her like a blanket. Attempting to put on a brave face while her leg throbbed proved more difficult than she had imagined; however, the pain paled in comparison to the pain of losing Rennie.

The party made her loss feel so real, cutting her to the quick. Anytime Lacey had found herself in a crowd as a youngster, Rennie had always been nearby. She had been her port in a storm, her comfort in a crisis. Her grandmother had always been there, and she had taken it for granted that she always would be. And now, with so many people coming up to her and offering condolences, there was no escaping the sad reality that the one person on earth who had offered unconditional love and understanding was gone.

She sighed, forcing back the tears, and glanced to the front of the room. She spied the large, smiling photo of her grandmother that had captured her attention several times since she'd arrived today. The photo had been taken just a year before. As she studied it again, she realized that Rennie had finally been showing her age.

Her grandmother had always looked younger than her years, but . . . the picture showed an older woman whose dark hair had morphed into a cap of bright white. Rennie had never resorted to coloring her hair, declaring that aging was a natural process and one that everyone should eagerly embrace. "What's the alternative?" she'd demand, and then she would break into a broad grin. "Death. That's the alternative."

It wasn't that Rennie was afraid of death, either. She said when her time came, she'd go out humming a tune. Had she? Lacey wondered. Had she left this earth smiling and ready to go? If only she had been there to bid her good-bye, to hold her hand, and to soothe her.

She shook her head, struggling to keep the tears at bay. She swallowed hard and stared even more intently at Rennie's photo. *Grandma, I miss you. I'm sorry.*

"Your grandmother was a wonderful woman."

She turned to the voice she recognized before her eyes actually lit on a face. "Pastor Wilson. It's nice to see you again."

"Well, it's nice to see you again too." He smiled sadly. "I wish we'd met again under different circumstances, Lacey Jane."

She nodded, meeting the older man's eyes. Although Pastor Wilson had to be seventy years old, his blue eyes still sparkled with youthful exuberance. Lacey had never been able to discern exactly how old the man was, because he'd been bald for as long as she could remember and had always had a smooth, rosy complexion. He wore spectacles that both enlarged his eyes and enhanced the intensity of the blue irises.

"Thank you for today's service . . . er, party," she said, grateful that Rennie's friends had put together such a festive farewell.

"It was my pleasure, and that of everyone else here," he assured her. "Rennie had so many friends. We're really going to miss her."

"Me too," she said wistfully, suddenly wishing Mason was nearby. She glanced around, spotted him, and somehow caught his eye as he stood talking to two men she didn't recognize. When he strode toward her, the men followed him and introduced themselves to her as deputies working under him at the sheriff's office.

She smiled politely through the introductions, but Mason didn't miss the anguish in her eyes. He bent to her ear. "Time to go?"

"Do you mind?" she asked.

"Not at all."

He rose and visually located his father across the room. "Dad," he called, and when he had his father's attention, gestured toward Lacey. Robert understood immediately that she was ready to go.

"Are you leaving, Lacey Jane?" Pastor Wilson asked with a frown. "I had hoped you and I could visit for a moment. It's been so long since I've seen you. I know several members of the congregation haven't had an opportunity to speak to you as yet. A few of us were just reminiscing about you earlier today."

She managed a tight smile. "Oh, well, I . . ."

The pastor suddenly laughed heartily and bent to pat her hand. "Oh, I will never forget you, Lacey Jane, five years old and marching yourself up to the—"

"Oh, please . . . ," she began, raising her hand to silence the exuberant pastor. "I'm sure you don't want to . . ."

"Tell the story?" he said, beaming. "Of course I do! You were so cute as you—"

Suddenly, another voice picked up the story—this one a female voice she soon realized belonged to Maureen Cartwright, the wife of the associate pastor and a longtime member of the church. The woman leaned close to her, smiling widely.

"You were so cute as you marched right up to the podium and jumped up and down, trying to reach the microphone. When you couldn't manage it, you gave up and announced—

loudly—that you knew your father was sitting somewhere in those pews and that he'd better stand up like a man and fess up."

Maureen grinned at her as she continued talking. "You said, 'Papa, I know you're out there. I'm five now, and time's a-wastin'. We'll just let bygones be bygones if you get up here right now.'"

The pastor laughed heartily, as did the rest of the group. Robert soon approached and glanced around, taking in Lacey's mortified face and the cheerful faces of everyone around her. Mason's face was the apparent exception. He appeared uncertain, since he sported a small, brief smile, before his features became marked with worry.

"What's so funny?" Robert asked, glancing from one face to another in the crowd that was rapidly growing.

Lacey sank lower in the wheelchair, but felt grateful when she heard another woman's voice, one she didn't recognize at first. It turned out to be Pastor Wilson's wife. "You're embarrassing her," Mrs. Wilson said sternly.

"Oh, Lacey Jane's not embarrassed, are you, dear?" Pastor Wilson said, the corners of his mouth twitching into a smile. He turned to Robert. "Remember how you strode calmly up those stairs to bring her down, when—"

Robert couldn't help slapping his thigh as he remembered how Lacey had led him across the sanctuary in a spirited chase. "That's right!" he enthused. "She yelled at the top of her lungs, 'I'm not going anywhere. Not till my papa fesses up!'"

Lacey covered her eyes with her hand, wishing the earth would swallow her up.

"And when Robert tried to talk to her, calmly asking her how she'd come to the conclusion that her papa was somewhere in those pews," said the pastor to the crowd, "she said she'd heard one of the church ladies—"

Suddenly, Mrs. Wilson jabbed her husband in the side with her elbow. She shook her head briskly when he gave her a puzzled stare. "Oh, *oh,* sorry," he mumbled.

Lacey knew why Mrs. Wilson wasn't eager for her husband to tell that particular part of the story. In truth, just prior to her animated announcement that fateful morning during the service, she had been downstairs, in the very same fellowship hall she was in now, helping Rennie prepare for an after-services buffet.

As she'd flitted around the room, she had spotted a lady with her hand to her mouth, obviously whispering to another lady. Since she couldn't very well bypass an opportunity to hear a secret, she had sidled up to the woman as inconspicuously as possible. She'd honed in on the woman's words like a guided missile.

"Somebody in this congregation was catting around," the first woman had said in a singsong voice, her lips pursed in a frown. "That child has a father around here somewhere, you mark my words. My best guess is he's sitting out there in one of those pews right now."

The other woman apparently hadn't been so keen on the gossip, since she had replied, "Lacey Jane's a darling little girl. Who her father is is neither here nor there to you or me—or to anyone else in this congregation."

"Well!" the other woman had said, aghast. "I was just saying . . ."

Lacey had heard enough. Her papa was in the congregation! Sitting out in one of those very pews. Well, she intended to find him that very moment!

She remembered the day as if it had been yesterday. In fact, stepping into the church today had been like stepping back in time. She recalled more of that horrible day. Robert had indeed called to her, asking her why she thought her father was there. It had been a question better left for later, he'd soon realized.

She had answered honestly, as small children do. "I heard a lady downstairs say my daddy is sitting out there somewhere." She had gestured grandly toward the openmouthed congregation. "The lady said he was cattin' around one day, but I guess he ain't cattin' around today, because she said he's probably here today. . . ."

Robert had made a successful grab for her then, scooping her into his arms and clamping a hand over her mouth. "Let's go have a little talk, you and me," Robert had said, as she had struggled against him. She remembered he had carried her outside, where the two had sat down and had indeed had that little chat. She nearly smiled at the memory. Almost.

Robert had told her any man would love to be the father of a little girl like her, and that he himself would have given his front teeth to have a little girl like her call him Papa. She had taken him at his word and had promptly begun calling him "Papa Robert" that very day. Rennie had tried to dissuade her, to no avail. Fortunately, Robert apparently hadn't minded, since he never made any attempts to stop her. As if it would have done him any good. In time, as she grew older, she had begun calling him "Pop."

She forced back a groan at the memories. She had been a handful, that much was certain. How had Rennie managed it? Losing a daughter, and left to care for a wild and wooly little granddaughter?

Her thoughts were interrupted by another member of the congregation, who had her own take on the events.

"I'll never forget my Beauford when he heard little Lacey Jane that day," said a woman she recognized as Alice Dupont, a longtime friend of Rennie's. "He had said, 'Hon, let's take her home.'" She chuckled at the memory. "You see, we have seven boys, had four then, and had been trying to have a little girl." She smiled wistfully. "Of course, Beauford said he wasn't real keen on the whole town thinking he'd been . . ." The woman giggled sheepishly. "Well, you know . . . But Beauford figured taking Lacey Jane on home would have saved him a whole lot of time and effort." Suddenly, Alice realized what she said, and let out a giggle. "Did I just say that?"

"Well, she was adorable," the pastor's wife spoke up. "Absolutely precious, but I think it's time we ended this stroll down memory lane. She's been through a lot and needs her rest."

If Lacey had had the ability to stand, she would have risen from the chair and wrapped her arms around Mrs. Wilson, right before she ran out of the church. She felt a splitting headache coming on that seemed to throb in synchronization with the pain in her leg. She sent a pleading glance at Mason, who took a step toward her.

Pastor Wilson took hold of Mason's arm. "Lacey Jane sure gave ol' Robert a run for his money that day," he said, still chuckling at the memory.

"Indeed she did," Robert agreed, smiling. "But then, she could always give us a run for our money. Remember when—"

Lacey sent Mason another imploring glance, but Mrs. Wilson came to her rescue again when she turned to Mason. "You should take her home. She isn't feeling well."

"Oh, Lacey's tough!" Robert declared.

Lacey resisted the urge to shoot Robert a dirty look. She knew he meant no harm, but still . . . Why was everybody always so bent on telling that story? And it looked as if he might tell another one. Good grief. Besides, to her mind, the story already told was a sad one. A little girl desperately seeking her father . . .

"I do think it's time I got her home," Mason said, his firm

voice leaving no room for argument. "Mrs. Wilson is right. She has been through a lot, and she's not feeling particularly well. She needs rest."

His eyes passed over Lacey's face, noting her features were drawn with fatigue and, likely, embarrassment. He'd have done anything to have spared her that humiliation. "Will you excuse us?" he asked the still-growing crowd.

"Of course," Mrs. Wilson said quickly, bending to give Lacey a reassuring smile. "You take care of yourself, dear. And please call me if you need anything."

Mason wheeled her outside, and she breathed in the fresh air. The air in the church's fellowship hall had felt stale and she just couldn't get a proper breath. Hearing the story of her childish antics had been a jolt—one she had probably forestalled as long as possible. She had known it was coming. It always did. The few times she'd returned to her small hometown, someone invariably brought it up.

"Are you all right?" Mason asked with concern. "You don't look so good."

"I forgot to take my pain pill in all the commotion of getting ready," she told him.

"Millie didn't give it to you?" he inquired, his eyebrows raised in surprise.

"She did," Lacey admitted. "But I put it down for just a minute to fix my necklace, and then forgot to take it."

He nodded and was silent for a moment. "Lacey, I'm sorry about what happened back there. I know that story bothers you. If it's any consolation, those people get a kick out of telling it because they really did think you were the cutest little thing they'd ever seen."

"It's all right," she said with a fatigued sigh. "Now that it's been told, maybe I won't have to hear it again."

"We'll get you home and into the recliner ASAP," he said,

lifting her out of the wheelchair and into the truck. He quickly stowed the wheelchair in back and then climbed into the cab. He gave her a worried look, and then draped an arm around her as he had done the last time they were in the truck together. This time she didn't resist, and before she knew it, she'd drifted off to sleep.

She woke when he was lifting her out of the truck. "You're going to hurt your back," she murmured sleepily.

"You let me worry about that," he said.

Chapter Ten

Monday morning, Mason knocked lightly on Lacey's door.

"Come in," she called in response.

"Hey, I have to stop by the office. I won't be long. Will you be okay?"

She nodded. "Millie is going to help me get ready," she said with a yawn.

"Good. Hey, do you feel like taking a walk later?"

"If you'd prefer, we could go jogging," she offered, mock-sweetly.

He rolled his eyes. "I meant, I'll walk and you'll ride in the wheelchair. I think a little fresh air might do you some good."

"Sure. Why not?" she said. A stroll through Mason's neighborhood might be nice.

Unfortunately, when he arrived home a short hour later and informed her that he'd already stowed her wheelchair in the bed of his truck, she realized he had other ideas about where they would be walking.

"Where are we going?" she asked as he deposited her in his truck. "Aren't we taking a walk around here?"

"No, I thought you might want to see the old town. Westover's really grown since you moved away." Before she could reply, he closed the door and rounded the truck. He climbed in and sent her a cheerful smile.

"Uh, Mason, I, uh . . ."

"What?" he asked as he started up the truck.

"I don't really need to see the town right now," she said. In fact, she didn't particularly care if she saw it at all. The more she thought about it, the more she realized she probably wouldn't be settling in Westover. With Rennie gone, there was no reason to stay. Of course, there was the matter of what to do with the house, which she knew her grandmother had left to her, but she didn't have to make any decisions about that now.

She was sentimental about it—it was her childhood home. But . . . did she really have the time or the inclination to renovate the house that was obviously in need of some major TLC? If only she could put the home on wheels and take it with her, but that wasn't a particularly realistic option. She would need a place to put it, and at present, she didn't have a plot of undeveloped land in her possession.

After she made inquiries about her father, and hopefully learned who he was and what had become of him, she would leave Westover again. She would likely keep in touch with Robert, and maybe even Mason, but her idea of contact meant an occasional e-mail or holiday card.

Mason ignored her protests about seeing the town, still declaring it would do her good to get out and socialize a bit. And he was eager to show her the new building housing the sheriff's office.

She wasn't happy about the forced visitation, but she couldn't do anything to stop the truck. When they arrived in town, and he parked alongside Main Street, she heaved a discouraged sigh.

"It won't be that bad," he said. "Hey, if you're good, I'll buy you an ice cream cone."

"Oh, hush up," she said, knowing Mason was once again alluding to their childhood.

As a little girl, she had been susceptible to the bribe of ice cream—any ice cream—to gain her cooperation. She could be throwing a screaming fit, and if Robert even mentioned ice cream, she would stop howling posthaste.

He chuckled as he climbed out of the truck and came to the passenger-side door. She considered locking the door, but knew that was decidedly childish behavior. She just wasn't interested in a look at the town, despite the fact that she hadn't stepped into the town proper since she'd left for college years before.

Once she was situated in the wheelchair, Mason draped a light jacket over her shoulders. "Are you comfortable?" he asked. "Warm enough? Hungry? Want that ice cream cone now?"

She took a deep, steadying breath. "If I wasn't in this chair, I'd clock you. Actually, come closer so I can."

"Why would you want to clock me?" he asked, his face the picture of innocence.

"You're treating me as if I'm an invalid. I'm not, by the way."

"Well, in a sense, you are," he pointed out. "If you're not *extremely* careful," he said, emphasizing the word, "you could do permanent damage to that leg. One false move and . . ."

Suddenly, his eyes widened. "Maybe I shouldn't have brought you out here." He glanced around. "Oh, shoot," he muttered. "What if a pedestrian accidentally bumps into you, or what if a small child runs into you and jars the leg, or what if—?"

"You're right," she said obligingly. "Maybe you should take me home, being as I'm in such a delicate state."

Mason ran a hand through his hair, clearly unsure what to do.

"Oh, for Pete's sake," she muttered. "Nobody is going to run into my doggone leg. And if they do, what can they really do to it? It's practically a bionic leg with all those spooky-looking pins. Besides, what kid would come near me with my leg looking like this?"

"It's not that bad," he said, "but just the same, we'll be careful."

Lacey found herself pushed along the broad sidewalk of Main Street. She didn't recall the downtown looking so polished and pristine, and made a comment to that affect.

"Oh, it's all part of our downtown revitalization project," Mason informed her. "Several new businesses opened up during the past year, including a couple of clothing boutiques and a small dog-grooming operation."

"That's nice," she said noncommittally.

"It is nice," he agreed. "For several years there, it looked like Westover was going to die a slow and agonizing death. The few businesses here were closing their doors in rapid succession, but . . . things are picking up lately."

"Well, that's good," she said.

"Yes, it is good," he said eagerly. "City Hall is doing everything it can to make Westover hospitable to business— particularly small business." Suddenly, his eyes narrowed as he studied her.

"What?" she demanded suspiciously.

"Don't suppose you've given any thought to hanging a shingle yourself?"

She laughed. "Not really."

"Why?"

She considered his question and then smiled lightly. "I'm accustomed to a certain pace."

"Yeah, well, that pace will kill you by the time you're fifty," he said testily. "There's something to be said for small-town life, Lacey, for a more sedate pace. There's something to be said for community and that sense of belonging you get living in a small town."

She nearly laughed out loud. "I never *belonged* here. Where've you been, Mason James?"

"Right here, Lacey Jane. Right here. If you'd bothered to keep up with me, you'd know that."

She felt a twinge of guilt. He and his father really were like family. She should have been more conscientious about staying in touch.

"And you did too belong here," he practically spat.

She registered an increase in his pace—likely in concert with his rising anger. "Mason," she said in measured tones, "I didn't belong. And would you slow down, please?"

"Like hell you didn't," he said in a taut voice, bringing the wheelchair to an abrupt halt and coming around to glare down at her surprised face. He shook his head vigorously. "I'll never understand you, Lacey Jane. All that talk over the years about not belonging. Of course you belonged. The only person who believed you didn't is *you!*"

She shook her head. "Not true," she said adamantly. "I was the fatherless kid running around in secondhand clothes—"

"Lacey Jane!" he scoffed. "Nobody thought of you as the 'fatherless' kid. As for you wearing secondhand clothes, my father—"

"Made sure I had new clothes," she cut in, and laughed without humor. "Yeah, I had new clothes because your dad bought them for me, and *everybody* knew it."

Mason stared into her face, his eyes flashing angrily. The green hue of his irises took on an emerald tone, liquid-bright and practically burning her face with their intensity. "Sometimes, I'd like to—"

"What?" she demanded. "What would you like to do? Here's an idea. Take me home—to your home—then pack my bags and take me *home*. Now there's something you can do for me."

He took a deep, shoring breath, and she suspected he was counting to ten. When a slow smile spread across his face, she felt hopeful he might just take her home. "Sorry," he said with a shrug of his broad shoulders. "You're not going anywhere. Like it or not, that leg is going to heal, and come hell or high water, or come the wrath of *you*," he added with chagrin, "I'm going to see that you walk on that leg without a trace of a limp."

Suddenly, she frowned. "Did Dr. Marks say I might have a limp?"

He realized he'd said too much. He took a deep breath. "Dr. Marks said if you don't do what you're supposed to do during your convalescence, then yes, you could end up with a limp. But you're going to do what you're supposed to do. I'm going to see to it."

She considered his words. A part of her wanted to give him a flippant response—tell him she didn't give a whit if she limped or not, that she could invest in a gem-studded cane and get along just fine, but . . . she wanted full use of the leg. Of course she wanted full use of the leg.

She appeared to sink resignedly into the chair, and Mason gave a small laugh of satisfaction. "There's a good girl."

She rose up slightly and glared at him. "Do . . . not . . . push . . . your . . . luck, Mason James," she warned, "because one day, I'll be out of this chair and—"

"Is that a threat?" he asked, biting back a smile. "Because it'll be a while before you can catch me, even when you get out of that chair."

"You just wait and see how easily I catch you when I'm motivated," she told him.

He stroked his jaw, and his eyes gleamed wickedly beneath arched brows. "And just what do you plan to do to me when you catch me?"

Taken aback, she wondered, was he flirting? If so, it wasn't the first time. "I already told you what I'd do," she said in a surly tone. "I'm going to clock you."

He smiled distractedly, and she could see the humor flee his eyes. "I'm glad to hear you're motivated, though, with respect to the leg," he told her, in all seriousness, "because you do have a long road ahead of you. That isn't a straightforward break you have there. You're going to have to work long and hard in physical therapy to get that leg back in shape."

She digested his words. The seriousness of the injury hadn't registered to that point. Rennie's sudden death had pushed all other concerns from her mind. She wondered, would she retain normal use of the leg? And what would it look like? Would she be disfigured? She told herself that a functioning leg was paramount, and that the appearance of the leg didn't matter. But she knew she was lying to herself. She wanted her leg back the way it was, before she'd made that fateful drive into town.

Drive into town. Into this town. She frowned. As she and Mason had driven into Westover, she hadn't thought about the intersection where she had been hit by the drunken kids. She glanced up ahead. She knew that intersection was several blocks ahead. If she saw it, would she remember the accident?

It was as if he read her thoughts. "Are you remembering something?" he asked. "About the accident?"

She shook her head. "No. I just realized I hadn't even thought about it, even as you drove me into town." She was silent for a moment, but finally spoke. "Frankly, Mason, I'm surprised you'd want to be in a vehicle with me." She shook her head ruefully. "We Karr women don't seem to have much luck when riding in cars."

He draped a hand across her shoulder, as he simultaneously leaned closer to give her what amounted to a hug. "I'm prepared to take my chances," he told her. "Just the same, I plan to continue to do the driving. I don't expect you'll be doing any driving for a good long while."

"That reminds me . . . My car . . . ?"

He winced. "Totaled is putting too positive a spin on it," he said with a grimace.

She sighed heavily. She had loved her little late-model car.

"Look on the bright side," he said. "Now you have your own personal chauffeur."

"And you have that personal job to get back to."

He shrugged good-naturedly. "I haven't taken a vacation since I started the job two years ago—"

"Why's that?" she cut in, watching him through narrowed eyes.

He shrugged again. "Just too busy, I guess."

Lacey cast another glance along the quiet street. It was absent of pedestrians other than the two of them. Very few cars had driven past. "Busy with *what?*" she asked with a chuckle.

"Don't let the silence fool you," he said mysteriously. "But enough shop talk." He continued pushing her wheelchair along Main Street.

When he paused in front of the ice cream shop, she shook her head. "I don't need ice cream."

"Well, I do."

He wheeled her into the shop, which featured a fifties retro theme. He approached the sleek, silver order counter, careful to assure Lacey was situated so her leg was out of the way of any incoming patrons.

"What'll you have?" he asked her.

She hadn't wanted ice cream until she'd seen the vast array of delectable choices beneath the glass cover.

"Well?" he prompted.

"I'll have . . . a scoop of boysenberry," she said, rising as much as she could manage and eyeing the creamy pink dessert in the large, round canister. "And . . . a scoop of chocolate brownie fudge. Oh, and strawberry cheesecake."

Mason eyed her for a few seconds. "I thought you didn't want ice cream," he said.

"That was until I actually *saw* the ice cream."

"Maybe you'd better put hers in a bowl," he told the young girl behind the counter.

"Yes," Lacey said, eyes sparkling. "And a few sprinkles on top wouldn't hurt," she added, gesturing toward the stacks of ice cream toppings on the counter.

He shook his head. "I'll have vanilla."

"Vanilla?" Lacey cried. "Vanilla! When you have all these choices?"

He shrugged. "What can I say?"

After he paid for their treats, he pushed her outside, careful to keep her leg out of harm's way. He took her to a bench, where he carefully positioned her chair, and then dropped onto the wooden seat. He leaned back, extending one muscular arm along the back and enjoying his cone with a contented sigh.

She attempted to relax, but she felt restless and unable to keep her unbroken leg from jumping up and down nervously. Mason spied the leg with a raised eyebrow. "Something wrong?" he asked. "Oh! Do you need to use the restroom?" He suddenly looked very uncomfortable.

"No, I don't need to use the bathroom. I'm not a toddler."

"Then why the jumpy leg?" he said, now grinning widely.

She sighed. "Just feeling fidgety. I'm not used to sitting still like this." She glanced around sleepy Main Street. "Really not much going on," she observed.

He weighed the remark with a nod. "As a law enforcement officer, I tend to like it when the town is quiet and everyone is doing what they should be doing."

"Do you get bored?" she asked. "I mean, I don't imagine there's much happening in Westover."

He cocked his head, appraising her with a glance. "No, I don't get bored. I'm actually a very busy man."

"Busy with what? I can't recall any crime sprees happening in Westover—at least I haven't seen anything on the news about anything particularly newsworthy. Tell me, what makes headlines in Westover?"

He stared at her intently, his mouth twitching into a sad, slow smile. "You," he said. "You made the paper, Lacey Jane."

Chapter Eleven

And this is my office," Mason told Lacey as he wheeled her into the large, utilitarian space.

"Nice," she said as she took in the serviceable desk with the padded leather chair behind it. Several plaques hung on the wall behind the desk, and she noted he had a nice view of Main Street below.

"Could be worse," Mason said, watching her face. "Probably doesn't compare to the opulence you're used to, though."

She laughed at that. "Opulence? I'm a lawyer, not a princess."

"You're trying to tell me you didn't work out of an exclusive suite in a high-rise building?"

"Well, I did work in a high-rise building; however, my office wasn't particularly impressive," she said. "Now, if I'd made partner . . ."

"Then your square footage would have increased."

"Sizably," she agreed.

"If your former employer were to offer to make you a partner now, would you accept?" he asked with interest.

"They did, and I don't know," she told him.

He eyed her quizzically. "You've been offered a partnership? You mean, since you came home?"

She nodded. "Since I came back *here*," she clarified. Portland was home.

"What do you plan to do?" He folded his arms across his

chest, watching her intently. "How would you manage it with the leg?"

"I wouldn't," she told him. "There's no way I can function in the way I did before, considering this bum leg. But when it heals—"

"Are they holding the position for you?" he interrupted.

She nodded. "So they tell me, but . . ."

"You don't put much stock in their promises?"

"No, not especially. My boss, Keith, had told me repeatedly that the job was mine, but it just didn't happen. He did suggest another type of partnership. . . ."

The instant Lacey divulged that to him, she regretted it. Why had she told him that? And why did it bother her so much that she'd told him?

From the hard glint in his eye, it was clear he was also bothered by the remark. He didn't speak, but instead rounded his desk and dropped heavily into the chair. He finally opened his mouth to speak, when a pretty brunet poked her head into the room. He clamped his mouth shut.

"You working, boss?" she asked.

"Not officially," he told her. "What's on your mind, Melissa?"

"Just needed you to sign off on some overtime sheets. Do you have a minute?"

He nodded his head and took the papers, hastily scrawling his signature on each sheet. He passed them back to the woman, and then proceeded to make introductions. "Melissa, this is Lacey Karr. Lacey, Melissa Taylor, my assistant."

The young woman extended a hand to Lacey. "It's nice to meet you."

"Likewise," she said, meeting the woman's eyes. What she saw there wasn't anything akin to nice. Although the woman had a smile on her lips, it didn't reach her eyes. She felt the hostility emanating from the woman's pretty features, and the room suddenly felt twenty degrees colder.

"So you're staying at Mason's place," the woman observed smoothly, and then laughed, turning toward him. "For the life of me, I just can't see Mason as a nursemaid."

"It's one of my many talents," he said, and Lacey could see by the stricken look in his eyes that he realized his remark could easily be misconstrued.

Melissa smiled smoothly, sidling up closer to him.

"Uh, I mean"—he cleared his throat and laughed—"I mean, Lacey and I practically grew up together. She's, er, *was,* like a cousin to me."

The woman eyed him quizzically, as did Lacey. She knew Melissa wondered what he meant by his remark, as did she. Why had he placed an emphasis on the *was?* So, she *was* like a cousin to him? What exactly was the nature of their relationship now? It was hard to discern from his words. Was he so fed up with her that he didn't think of her in such friendly terms, or . . . ?

She knew she still rubbed Mason the wrong way and had sensed some tension between them on several occasions. She gulped. Was he seeing her differently? She couldn't deny she was seeing him through different eyes.

"Well, it's nice of you to help your old friend," Melissa said, dismissing her altogether now. "So," she asked, addressing Mason, "when do you plan to return to work full time? This place is falling apart without you."

"Oh, I doubt that," he said, but Lacey could see he was pleased to hear it.

"Well?" Melissa prompted, grinning widely.

Lacey noted she was a pretty girl, with gleaming brown hair and large brown doe eyes. The blue uniform she wore did little to hide her curves. She wondered, was Mason involved with this woman?

And if so, why did it bother her? What did she care if he was involved with her? Really, he was like a cousin—or maybe even a brother. An annoying relative . . . Well, maybe not so annoying . . . Not so much a cousin . . . Definitely not a brother. Lacey gulped. Oh, brother.

She shook her head, hoping neither Mason nor the brunet had noticed the odd, jerking shake of her head. It was as if she'd attempted to shake the thought out of her brain—as if the thought of him being involved with this woman simply could not compute in her mind. Frankly, none of her thoughts were computing.

She turned and glanced out the window. She gulped loudly again. What the heck was wrong with her? If she didn't know better, she'd think she was jealous. But that was ridiculous. Too ridiculous to contemplate.

When she turned back and saw Mason give Melissa a high-voltage smile in response to something she'd said, Lacey felt a wave of emotion cascade over her. And there was no mistaking this time what the emotion was. She was jealous, and green with it. Oh, brother.

"You're awfully quiet, Lacey," Mason observed as he pushed her out of his office.

"Oh, uh, just tired," she said.

"Oh, shoot," he said, "I forgot something. Sit tight, okay? I'll be right back."

She had no choice but to sit tight, she thought ruefully. He had left her beside a water fountain, her leg parallel to the wall. She felt like an ungainly piece of wall art. She glanced around, taking in her surroundings.

In front of her was a long hallway, with doors lining the

length of it. Behind her was a circular area, ringed with elevators, and directly beside her was a partition, which appeared to be one of many dividing a very large interior space.

"She doesn't seem like his type."

The female voice startled her, seeming to originate from behind the partition nearest to her. She glanced up curiously, wondering, were they talking about her?

When the woman continued talking, Lacey registered that the voice belonged to Melissa, the woman she had just met. She heard the woman laugh, the sound like tinkling ice. "I just wonder exactly what kind of *nursing* Mason is up to," she said coolly.

"Oh, I can just imagine," the other woman said. "I'm telling you, Melissa, the man is partial to blonds."

She chortled. "Well, as you well know, I aim to cure him of that." She laughed seductively. "Or, I could always go blond. I wonder if it's true they have more fun." She laughed again, but sobered. "I can't imagine what Sheriff James sees in that woman, anyway," she said unkindly. "Particularly since, from what I understand, her leg is really messed up. I hear she may never walk again without the use of a cane. He'd be stuck taking care of an invalid."

Lacey let out a sharp breath. How dare these women talk about her! They didn't know her. And they certainly didn't know the details of her injury. Her, an invalid? Hardly.

She almost spoke up, but bit back the words when she realized how embarrassing it would be to confront these women if there were others working within those partitions.

"You know who she is, don't you?" the other woman said, taking her voice down a notch.

"What do you mean?" Melissa asked. "Mason said she was like a cousin to him, that they'd grown up together."

"She's Rennie Karr's granddaughter," the woman said

conspiratorially. "Her mother abandoned her years ago. No one knows who her father is, and I understand that Mason's father had to practically support the family. They were dirt poor. . . ."

Lacey hadn't registered that Mason had come up beside her and heard the latter part of the women's conversation. She turned toward him when she sensed his presence, but by then he had already stridden toward the gossiping women.

"Ladies," she heard him say, "something on your minds?"

"Oh, no, no, Sheriff," the other woman said.

"Oh, no, nothing," Melissa said as she popped her head out from behind the partition. Her eyes widened when she spotted Lacey, who managed to keep her face impassive. It was a talent she had developed during her teenage years, and then perfected as a lawyer.

"Are you sure?" he asked.

When both women said yes, he spun on his heel and returned to Lacey. He promptly wheeled her away from the women. He suspected their comments had left her mortified and embarrassed. He also suspected they had likely cemented her resolve that she couldn't trust anyone in this town—that the population of Westover still viewed her as the offspring of one of the town's most infamous occupants. The reality made him want to throttle his employees for their insensitivity. He also wanted to take Lacey into his arms and comfort her, but he knew she wouldn't like it one bit. Heck, half the time he suspected she didn't like *him* one bit.

It didn't diminish the fact that he had wanted to soothe and protect her, but he knew that had he responded to the women's comments, she would have been outraged. Anytime he had come to her defense when they were children, she had railed against his interference. He knew she was only accepting his help now because she had no other choice and that she wasn't particularly happy to be in his home. She had always insisted on independence, on fighting her own battles.

Outside the building, as he was lifting her into the truck, Mason attempted to catch her gaze. She studiously ignored him as he situated her in the cab. He climbed in, unspeaking, and started the ignition. She remained quiet during the drive home.

As much as he wanted to speak to her, he kept quiet. As frustrated as he was that his employees had been gossiping and had said mean-spirited things about Lacey and her family, he couldn't bring himself to rise to the level of anger he knew she was likely experiencing.

Perhaps he was simply an easygoing guy, but he knew that humans are that—human. That they speak out of turn, bear false witness, and in general, make mistakes. He didn't excuse or condone these women's behavior, and he was arguably disappointed by it, but their words didn't have real power. Their only power was what Lacey gave to them.

He often wondered, and still did, why she worried so much about what others thought of her. Growing up, didn't she know that she was the girl all the other girls had wanted to emulate? Didn't she realize her blond beauty had made the guys go weak in the knees, and that they had fallen all over themselves to get her attention? He knew half a dozen guys who had wanted to marry her. Of course, he'd seen to it that they hadn't gotten within ten feet of her. . . .

He raked a hand through his hair. "Uh, Lacey," he began tentatively, "I hope you're not going to . . ."

"Not going to what?" she asked.

"Not going to take those women seriously. What they were engaging in is called gossip, idle chitchat, something most humans are guilty of now and again, and . . . their words only have power if you let them."

"Geez, you sound like some positive-thinking guru. By the way, spare me."

He chuckled. "I've always been a 'glass is half full' kind of a guy," he said with a shrug.

"And I've—"

"Always been a 'don't drink the water—it's poison!' kind of a girl," he cut in, laughing loudly and seeming pleased with himself.

She shot him a disgusted look. She chose not to respond. She was too tired to respond. How had she ended up back in Westover, hardly a blip on *anyone's* radar? How had she become trapped in the last place on earth she wanted to be?

She sighed heavily, thinking that if she'd arrived at that Main Street intersection a fraction of a second sooner or later, she'd be whole. She'd have made it to Rennie's bedside, and she would have said good-bye to her beloved grandmother. She would have planned her grandmother's farewell party, and then bid Westover a final farewell herself.

"What are you thinking, Lacey?"

She simply shook her head.

"Tell me," he prompted.

She met his gaze, albeit briefly, before she turned to face out the passenger window.

"Lacey?"

She decided to tell him the truth. "I was thinking, if I had arrived at the intersection even a fraction of a second sooner or later, I wouldn't be stuck in this town. And you wouldn't be stuck with me," she said, her voice breaking.

"Someone's feeling sorry for herself," he said.

"Shut up."

He surprised her when he pulled over to the side of the road. He turned off the ignition, and then shifted in the seat and wrapped her in his arms. She didn't have the strength to struggle against his imprisoning arms, and wasn't sure she even wanted to if she could. She felt herself pulled tighter against his broad, muscular chest, and smelled his clean, masculine scent.

She closed her eyes, suddenly dizzy from the heady reality of something she couldn't quite wrap her mind around. Something she refused to wrap her mind around. Unbidden, the thought came anyway. *This feels right.*

His voice brought her out of her troubling thoughts. "Lacey, it's ridiculous to care what those women had to say."

She wasn't thinking about those women or their words. Frankly, she realized, she didn't really care what those women had to say about her. It was an epiphany. If they'd spoken about her like that when she'd been an impressionable teen, she'd have been devastated. But now, she really couldn't have cared less. What she did care about was the realization that she needed to get out of Westover, and not just because she abhorred the town she remembered from her youth.

She needed to get out of town because she realized she had feelings for Mason. Mason James, the bane of her existence and the closest thing to a cousin she had ever had. When Melissa had eyed Mason as if he were a piece of meat, ready to be put on the skewer of her own private barbecue, Lacey had felt such an intense jolt of jealousy, she felt embarrassed for it. And she couldn't help wonder, what did it mean?

Chapter Twelve

Hey, Lacey, I forgot to tell you yesterday that I attempted to contact the college your mother attended."

Mason had her rapt attention. She glanced up from the book she was reading and snapped it closed. "Did you find out anything?" she asked eagerly.

He sighed and shook his head. "It's just what I thought. They have strict privacy laws."

"But you're a sheriff," she said, surprised. "They wouldn't give *you* the information?"

"I did identify myself, but in fairness to them, they had no way of knowing if I'm legit or not over the telephone. Anybody can say they're anything, and there's no way to know the truth of the matter over the phone."

She acknowledged his words with a nod of her head. "What can we do?"

He smiled briefly, despite the solemnity of their conversation. She had said "we" rather than "I." It gave him reason to hope.

"Well," he said, "I plan to send off a fax tomorrow morning. I'm hoping if the college's admissions office sees the Westover Sheriff's Department letterhead, they'll be more inclined to help us."

"And if they won't?"

"We'll pay them a visit."

She leaned forward in the chair. "Soon?"

He dropped into the nearby loveseat. "After Dr. Marks gives you the all-clear to travel."

She shot a disgusted glance at her leg. Although it wasn't nearly as painful as it had been, it was still encased in the high-tech splint with the nausea-inducing pins.

"It won't be long," Mason said. "You're getting stronger every day."

"But is the leg?" she wondered aloud.

"Well, we'll know more tomorrow. You have an appointment with Dr. Marks at two thirty."

"You're starting back to work tomorrow, aren't you?" she asked.

"Nope, not until Monday. I'll be going with you to the appointment."

"You don't have to," she said tiredly. "You've done . . ." She paused, searching his face. "You've done so much for me already."

A slow smile spread across his face. "It's not a problem," he said sincerely. "You know how much I . . . care about you."

A lingering silence followed, since Lacey was uncertain what to say in return. Yes, he cared about her, like a cousin, or perhaps like a brother cared for a sister, right? Then why did she have a feeling there was more to the story?

To diffuse the sudden tension between them, she reached for a pillow beside her on the recliner and hefted it at him. It thumped against his head. A broad smile creased his face. "Why, if you weren't injured . . . ," he threatened.

"I'd still kick your butt in a pillow fight," she said, a challenging glint in her eye.

He smiled, tilting his head to the side as he studied her.

"Yeah, Lacey, you'd probably still kick my butt in most anything."

"And don't you forget it," she threatened with a grin.

"Where's Mason?" Lacey asked later that afternoon. She'd fallen asleep, and awoke to Millie puttering around the family room, tidying up.

"Oh, dear, did I wake you?" her friend asked with concern.

"No, no, I've been sleeping long enough anyway," she answered with a yawn.

"Do you need anything, dear?" Millie asked.

"Not a thing," she assured her.

Millie paused, hands on hips. "Honey, you have to be the easiest patient I've ever tended to."

Lacey chuckled. "I don't know about that."

"You never ask for a thing. Just so you know, dear, you're not imposing if you ask me for help. It's my job to take care of you."

"And you're doing an excellent job, Millie," she assured her. "I don't know what I would have done without you over the past weeks."

Suddenly, both women glanced toward the front of the house when they heard the doorbell ring. "I'll get that," Millie said, and hurried off.

She soon returned with Donna Tipton in tow, Lacey's best friend from high school.

She glanced at her former friend uncertainly, since she was so surprised to see her. Finally, she found her voice. "Donna Tipton, is that really you?"

"In the flesh," her friend said, and then spread her arms wide. "And there's a lot of flesh here," she joked.

Lacey laughed. "You look great," she assured her, and then turned to Millie. "This is Donna, my best friend from high school."

The two women exchanged pleasantries, and then Lacey invited Donna to sit down. When it appeared Millie was going to head to the bedroom to do some cleaning, Lacey called her back in. "Millie, join us."

Millie turned and smiled, and Lacey gave an encouraging nod.

"Before I sit, coffee, anyone?" Millie asked.

"I'd love a cup," Donna said, but then patted her expanding belly. "But I'm off caffeine for a while." She grinned. "Two more months, to be exact. And mind you, I'm counting the days, hours, and minutes."

"Is there something else I can get you?" Millie asked. "Water, milk, juice . . . ?"

"Water would be great," Donna said, and Millie looked at Lacey.

"Sounds good to me as well," she said.

Millie was back in a flash with glasses of water for all, and the three women began visiting.

"Lacey, I can't believe you've come home," Donna said, grinning. "Frankly, I didn't think you'd ever come home to settle."

"Oh, uh, well," she stammered, "I haven't . . ."

Donna looked disappointed. "You're not going to stay?"

Lacey shook her head and shrugged. "I haven't made any plans as yet," she explained.

"Oh, I was hoping you would stay," she said. "I've missed you."

"I'm sorry I didn't keep in touch."

"Hey, I could have tried to reach you too. But you know how it is—life sort of takes over. In my world, there's hardly a minute in the day that isn't filled with activity."

"With three kids and one on the way, I can imagine," Lacey commiserated.

"So you heard about my brood?"

She nodded.

"All boys," she grinned ruefully. "Can you imagine that? Lord knows I couldn't have imagined it." She patted her belly. "I'm praying for a girl."

"Oh, I hope you get her!" Millie cried. "Every woman needs a daughter."

"They're more loyal than boys when they grow up," Donna said, "or at least that's what *everybody* insists on telling me." She laughed. "I hope I get the chance to find out."

"So you don't know the sex of the baby?" Lacey asked.

Donna shook her head. "No, Chet and I always prefer to wait for the surprise. If it's a boy, it isn't as if we need to do any shopping. I have just about everything I need for a little boy."

"If it's a girl . . . ," Millie said.

"Then I need to shop. But I'll be happy either way. I love my boys." Donna gave Lacey a speculative glance. "How about you? Do you have any children?"

She shook her head vigorously. "Oh, no, I'm not married."

Donna nodded. "Any man in your life?" She chuckled. "I think half the boys at Westover High planned to marry you, but you showed them all by leaving town before the ink could dry on your diploma."

Lacey shifted in the chair. "The boys?" She shook her head. "I wasn't aware . . ." She smoothed a hand over her hair. "None of the boys—"

"Oh, come on," her friend scoffed. "You know very well that you were the most popular girl in school."

She gave her a puzzled glance. "I wasn't popular. I—"

Donna turned to Millie. "She never realized how beautiful she is, either." She laughed then, but grew silent, as if recalling an event from her past. "Lacey, do you remember when that boy asked you to wear his number at the big game? I think his name was Jake Colton."

She fought to keep from pressing her eyelids together. The memory of that humiliation still burned in her brain, particularly since she and Mason had talked about it so recently. "I remember."

Donna turned to Millie. "The boy had a girlfriend, but he thought she was going to be out of town for the weekend of the big game. Since he had a crush on Lacey, he figured he'd ask her to wear his number, and then, if she did, he intended to dump his girlfriend later."

"Cad!" Millie said good-naturedly.

"Anyway, his girlfriend had a change of plans and showed up at the game. She saw Lacey wearing her boyfriend's number on a T-shirt, and boy howdy, the girl was fit to be tied."

Lacey smiled wanly in memory. "I didn't know he had a girlfriend," she said in defense. "He was the first boy to express an interest in me."

"He was the first boy bold enough to approach you, considering . . ."

"Considering what?" Lacey asked, frowning.

"Oh, come on," Donna said, her eyes alight with humor.

"What?" Lacey prompted. "Considering what?"

"Considering that Mason James was madly in love with you, so much so that he warned off every other boy anytime he heard a rumor someone might be interested in you."

"Mason . . . didn't . . . uh . . . ," she stammered. "He couldn't stand me," she insisted.

"Lacey! Mason was so in love with you, *he* could hardly stand it."

Millie chuckled, clapping her hands together gleefully. "I knew it! I knew it. Our sheriff is in love with Lacey."

"He is not!" Lacey cried, aghast.

"Oh, he was, and probably still is, then," Donna said, sending a clarifying glance at Millie, who nodded in return and mouthed, "I think so."

Donna continued, "Anyway, when Mason found out Jake Colton asked Lacey to wear his number, he . . . was . . . furious. He tracked Jake down, gave him what for, and then hurried to find her."

"Then he asked me to wear *his* number," Lacey said, pointedly and angrily. "Can you imagine that?"

Donna gave her a puzzled glance. "What do you mean?"

"He knew I'd just been humiliated by Jake, and then he decided to add insult to injury by embarrassing me again."

"How?"

"By asking me to wear his number," she said succinctly.

Donna watched her as if she'd taken leave of her senses. "Lacey, Mason asked you to wear his number because he was in love with you. He had heard about the other kid and was doubly furious because he'd already intended to ask you to wear his number. The other kid beat him to the punch."

"Why did he want me to wear his number?" she asked, her brows furrowed in a puzzled frown.

"Because he loved you!" Millie and Donna cried in unison.

"No, no," Lacey asserted. "He wanted to embarrass me too."

"He did not," Donna said. "He felt horrible about that other boy and his girlfriend and her friends embarrassing you, and if he hadn't had other fish to fry—namely asking you to wear his number—he would have pummeled the kid."

"Mason wasn't the violent type," Lacey said distractedly, remembering that Mason had always been one to solve problems by talking things out. She was the one who had always been tight-lipped.

"Lacey!" Donna cried, pulling her from her reverie. "Mason

was in love with you. He confided in me after his number-wearing request went sour. He told me he didn't know what he'd done wrong, and he felt terrible." She grinned. "You should have seen him, all lovesick and miserable."

"No way," she said. "It's not possible."

"And why isn't it possible?"

"Because he and I were always so . . . so . . . antagonistic toward each other. We got on each other's last nerve."

"Then it was true love," Millie teased with a laugh. "When a young boy and girl clash, it's usually a sign of chemistry between them."

"Oh, yeah, sure," Lacey said. "Antagonism equates to chemistry. Conjures up all sorts of romantic notions."

"What conjures up all sorts of romantic notions?" Mason's voice came loud and clear from behind the women.

"Nothing," Millie said, glancing at the others in alarm.

"Nothing," Donna echoed crisply, shaking her head.

"Nothing at all," Lacey murmured, failing to make eye contact with him.

He gave the women a sweeping, speculative glance, but his eyes settled on Lacey. "Okaaay then," he said with a chuckle, as he turned and left the room.

Chapter Thirteen

Lacey shot Mason a speculative glance, her eyes passing over his face. "What's up?" he asked. "You've been giving me funny looks since your friend left."

He rose up from his reclining position on the couch and swung his legs over the side. He stretched lazily, his lean muscles rippling beneath the thin fabric of his T-shirt.

"Uh, nothing," she assured him. "Nothing at all." She averted her eyes.

When had he become so good-looking? Did he work out? Clearly he worked out.

"No, really, what gives?" he persisted. "You seem preoccupied."

"Oh, nothing."

"If you weren't wounded, and we were still kids, I'd be sitting on you right now, giving you the tickle torture until you talked," he said.

"Yeah, that's what you think," she scoffed. "Before you managed to pin me, I'd have done my famous pit-pull maneuver and stretched your arm from here to Sunday."

Mason absently rubbed his underarm, apparently remembering Lacey's personal brand of torture.

Since he had been taught never to hit a girl, she had preyed upon the gentlemanly weakness at every turn. She had often pummeled him into submission, so that she could get him on the ground, sit on him, and shove her foot into his armpit. Once positioned, she had pulled on his arm with both her hands until he had begged for mercy. It was cruel and unusual punishment, and she had delighted in wielding it.

"You were an awful, awful girl," he mused, watching her as if seeing her as the little terror she had been.

"See, I knew it!" she said triumphantly.

"Knew what?" he asked, still rubbing the ghost pain in his arm.

"Oh, nothing," she said quickly.

"Oh no you don't," he said, rising from the couch and coming to stand beside the recliner. "You started this. Now talk."

She laughed, and it sounded forced to her own ears. "Let's just drop it."

"Talk!" Mason commanded.

"Okay, look, it's silly, but . . ."

"Yeah?" he said with frustration.

"Donna has this ridiculous idea that, well, at some point . . ."

"What?"

"That you, kind of, well, sort of . . ."

"Lacey, I'm starting to think your closing arguments in court must be awfully weak," he observed. "Uh, ladies, and uh, well, uh, gentlemen of the, uh, jury . . ."

"Oh, shut up!" she said, but couldn't help laughing.

"Okay, I'll shut up, but you talk."

"Okay, look, Donna has this odd notion that you, well . . ."

He gave her a pointed look.

"Okay! She said you had a crush on me once upon a time."

"Well, it looks as if Donna can't keep a secret," he said with mock indignation.

Lacey chuckled nervously. "She kept it for eleven years. So it's true?"

He weighed her words with a side-to-side movement of his head. "Okay, she keeps a secret better than most," he acknowledged, but didn't answer her question.

"So you . . . ?"

"Oh, come on," he interrupted, watching her with a hint of a smile. "You knew how I felt about you."

She shook her head, her brows furrowed over genuinely puzzled eyes. "Mason, I . . ."

He laughed, a deep, throaty chuckle, but then sobered. "I'll tell you what, Lacey Jane. For me, the sun set on that blond head of yours. Heck," he added ruefully, "you were the sun." He arched his brows, crossed the room, and left. She had no idea where he went.

If Lacey had had any means of leaving the house, she would have walked out then. Not to leave, but to search for Mason. When he told her how he had felt about her all those years ago, he had smiled, but she could see something beyond the forced good humor. Had she . . . hurt him?

Lord knew she hadn't wanted to hurt him—ever. Not *really* hurt him. Well, she had wanted to inflict physical pain—hence the pit pull, but she hadn't ever wanted to inflict emotional pain. She hadn't even meant to hurt him when she was competing against him in the academic arena in high school.

In fact, when she had managed to accumulate enough credits to graduate high school early, and had been told by her guidance counselor that her 4.0 grade-point average had earned her the right to give the commencement speech to the senior class, she had declined. Mason had had a GPA of 3.97, and she hadn't wanted to take from him the honor of giving that speech. And he had spoken eloquently, nearly bringing tears to her eyes at the time.

She felt tearful and emotional now. How had she not recognized that he cared about her—that he saw her as more than the little girl who had annoyed him at every turn?

Although it was ancient history and irrelevant now, she still felt a twinge of guilt that she had been so driven—so single-minded—that she had missed something that must have felt important to him at the time. She had no illusions. She knew adolescents felt things deeply and that what they felt was very real to them. As easy as it was to dismiss the youthful angst of adolescence, for many, it didn't diminish the pain of those years. And Lacey had had her own brand of pain. She'd worked tirelessly to excel, and for one reason only—as a means to escape Westover and all the whispers.

When Mason finally came back to the family room, he dropped onto the couch without a word. He didn't flip on the TV, but simply lay there, apparently resting his eyes, or intent on falling asleep.

"Mason," she said softly. "Are you sleeping?"

"Nope," he said.

"Do you want to talk?"

"About what?" he asked obtusely.

"Where've you been?"

"Outside. Thinking."

"To the trees?"

"Yep."

"And what were you thinking about?" she asked.

He rose up then, swinging his legs over the side of the couch in an easy motion. "You," he said.

"Me?"

"Yep." He broke into a wide grin. "So, you really didn't know how I felt about you in high school?"

She shook her head. "I had no idea."

"None?" he said, his brows furrowed. "Really?"

"Really."

"Well, you were pretty focused on your studies," he observed.

"Apparently," she said. "Mason?"

"Yeah?"

"Maybe I should stay somewhere else?"

"Why?"

"Well, I mean . . ."

"Lacey, my infatuation with you back then does not have any bearing on today."

"But . . ." She felt a vague sense of disappointment.

"But nothing. We're like family, and you're not going anywhere. At least not until that leg is better."

"Are you sure?"

"Yes," he told her.

"Mason?"

"Yeah?"

"Thanks."

Later that evening, Mason announced he was going to bed early. Millie had already helped Lacey get ready for bed, but Lacey was interested in a television show and decided to stay up to finish watching it, and then sleep in the recliner.

"Suit yourself," Mason said, and headed upstairs.

She settled in to watch the program. Her mind wandered often, as she thought about her adolescent years in Westover. How had she missed that Mason had feelings for her then? It still grieved her to think she had hurt him. As aggravating as the boy had been, and as frustrated as she could get with him now, he had certainly stepped up to the plate to help her. She realized how much he had done for her, altering his life to accommodate her and her injury. She knew she owed him a huge debt of gratitude.

She would have to express that to him before she left his home. And if need be, she would return the favor, should the need ever arise.

She finally focused on the television again, and realized with surprise that her program had ended. She glanced around her, but couldn't see the remote. She patted the gaps in the chair, but still couldn't find it. In the dim light, she spotted the remote across the room on the couch. It might as well have been a mile away. She couldn't get to it.

Her inability to reach it wouldn't have been a problem, were it not for the movie that had just begun playing on the set. It was a horror movie—one she hadn't wanted to see when it had come out in theaters. Particularly frightening, the movie featured a young woman alone in a house that happened to pulse with a life of its own. As the movie progressed, Lacey attempted to shut her eyes and fall asleep. Unfortunately, she suspected she might never sleep again.

She peered at the set through one eye, pressing it closed when a terrifying scene came on. She kept her eyes closed, until . . . Just a peek, she thought.

Should have kept my eyes closed!

Lacey slumped down in the chair, desperately wishing she had two functioning legs. If only she had asked Mason to pass her the remote. She ventured a glance at the TV, and promptly stuffed her hand over her mouth to keep from screaming.

Fortunately, she had a large blanket covering her, and opted to throw it over her head. She attempted to talk herself down from the fear. *You're a grown woman. A professional. You've lived alone for years. This is a movie. A B movie at that. It is not real. It is through the magic of Hollywood that that house appears to ooze blood. . . .*

The pep talk wasn't working, and she forced herself to take

a deep, steadying breath. She would just have to watch the movie when she could take it, close her eyes when she couldn't, and hope it ended soon.

To her horror, when another scary scene flashed across the screen, she let out a scream. She startled herself, and then wondered, had she been loud? Did she wake Mason up? If she did, was it really a bad thing at this point?

Yes, she realized, it would be awful to wake him. He needed his sleep. He'd been carrying her all over town, and she knew he needed all the rest he could get. However, to her surprise, he came bounding down the steps off the family room. She could see the fear in his eyes, despite the limited lighting in the room.

"What's wrong?" he demanded, his eyes passing over her face.

"Did I wake you?"

He gave her a puzzled glance. "Yeah, you screamed."

"Was I loud?" she asked, wincing apologetically.

He shook his head. "I don't know." He held up something she couldn't readily identify.

"What's that?"

"Monitor," he said, and then yawned.

Lacey watched him, curious. "What?" she asked, shaking her head in puzzlement.

"I have a monitor, so I can hear you if you should need me in the night. I heard you," he finished lamely when he registered the horrified expression on her face.

"A baby monitor! Dang it, Mason, you should have told me!" she cried, mortified to think he had been able to hear her as she slept.

"Why?" he asked, raking a hand through his hair. He watched her, sleepy-eyed and shirtless, and it was the latter that caused her to nearly forget she was angry. When he wiped a hand across his torso, she swallowed hard. He had a six pack the likes of which she hadn't seen before.

"Um, what was the question?" she muttered numbly, and then spotted the monitor again. "Oh, yeah, that! Mason, do you mean to tell me you can hear me when I'm sleeping?"

"Well, yeah," he said, "but usually I'm sleeping too."

"But you can hear me . . ."

"Precisely," he said, seemingly waking up a bit. "What's the problem?"

"Geez, Mason . . . Do I snore?" she asked, hedging for his answer.

He broke into a grin. "Like a logger."

"I do not!"

He cocked his head to the side and scrubbed at his jaw. "Sometimes you sound more like a freight train building up speed."

"I'm moving out tomorrow," she threatened, thoroughly embarrassed to think he had the capacity to hear whatever noises she made in her sleep. Good lord, did she talk in her sleep?

"Do I talk in my sleep?" she demanded shrilly, giving him a beseeching glance.

"Oh, yeah," he said without hesitation.

"What do I say?"

"I don't know. You keep saying something about . . ."

"What?" she shrieked.

"Oh, uh, something about . . ."

"Something about what?" she demanded. "Mason, don't make me come over there."

"As if you could," he mocked.

"Mason, tell me!"

"You keep muttering something about me being the man of your dreams." He shrugged his broad shoulders. "Yeah, I think that's it."

"In *your* dreams!" she cried.

"Maybe," he conceded good-naturedly, with a shrug and a yawn. "What are you doing up?"

"You left the remote on the couch," she accused.

"Yeah, so? Oh! You couldn't turn the TV off." He gave a self-effacing shrug. "Sorry."

"Nor could I change the channel," she said pointedly.

He glanced at the set. "You don't like horror movies. Oh!" He stood frozen, watching a particularly horrifying scene. "Oh," he repeated numbly. He turned back to her. "Will you ever be able to sleep again? I know how you used to hate horror movies. Remember that one time—"

She waved him quiet, frustrated. "I don't want to talk about it."

"Okay, I'll turn off the set and let you get some sleep."

"Uh, Mason . . ."

"Yeah?"

"I'm kind of into the movie now."

"You want to see the ending?" he asked incredulously.

"I . . . think so."

"And you want me to stay in here with you," he said knowingly.

She nodded. "Do you mind?"

He muttered all the way to the couch. He lay down, putting his arm under his head to lift himself up for a good view of the TV. He glanced over at Lacey periodically, noting she was glued to the set, her eyes wide and a hand to her mouth.

When yet another frightening scene came on, she attempted to curl her legs up, but couldn't. Ridiculously, it occurred to her that the toes on her broken leg were exposed, unprotected against . . . Oh, her imagination was getting the better of her.

She shook herself. She was being ridiculous. She saw that Mason had turned away from the set and was watching her instead. She was a bundle of nerves. He, on the other hand, simply yawned as if bored. She turned back to the movie.

"Lacey, the critics panned this movie. Are you sure you want to finish it?"

She nodded without looking at him, unable to pull her eyes from the screen. He continued to watch her, smiling. Was this the same cool, professional, self-reliant beauty who had moved into his home a couple of weeks before? He couldn't help laughing when he noticed she kept trying to look behind her, as if she thought something might grab her from behind. He knew he ought to turn off the set, to save her from herself, but he opted for a different course of action.

He rose from the couch, crossed the room, and lifted her out of the recliner. He carried her to the couch. She was so engrossed in the movie, she could only briefly stare, stupefied, at him as he carefully raised the leg rest on the recliner sofa to support her cast. He hurriedly retrieved an ottoman, so he'd have a place for his feet, and then settled in next to her. She didn't speak, even as he wrapped an arm around her and pulled her close. She didn't seem to register his closeness until a commercial came on. She glanced from him to the TV and back, several times. Apparently, she'd lost the power of speech, or she was simply antsy for the movie to come back on.

When it did, she turned back toward the set, as if pulled by an invisible string. As each scene on TV played out, she settled in closer to Mason, unaware she was doing so. He simply held her tighter, and chuckled whenever she burrowed her face in his chest. Was this woman really Lacey Jane Karr? She couldn't be.

Chapter Fourteen

Lacey woke up slowly, realizing that her body felt oddly stiff and uncooperative. She attempted to stretch, but for some reason couldn't. Her eyes fluttered open and she glanced up to see Mason smiling down into her face.

For a brief couple of seconds, she was disoriented. Why was she on the couch, wrapped in his arms? And then she remembered.

"Oh," she said aloud.

He chuckled. "I'm afraid you're going to need a night-light from here on out."

She smiled sheepishly. "You're probably right."

When she didn't make a move to extract herself from his arms, he couldn't help but wonder why. He had expected her to wake up, see him, and then scream. It was certainly what the Lacey of old would have done. Instead, she simply remained nestled in his arms, but then, he realized, it wasn't as if she could go anywhere.

With that sobering realization, he eased himself off the couch, careful to keep from jostling her leg. "How do you feel?" he asked.

"Stiff."

He glanced at the clock across the room. "Millie should be here any minute. Do you want to go to your room?"

"Yes, if you don't mind, I'd like to go to *your* room," she clarified with a soft smile.

"Uh-huh."

He easily lifted her, and she resisted the urge to rest her face against his neck. She fought the desire to reach out and stroke the stubbled planes of his face. She gasped at her own audacity, and he eyed her, curious. "What's up?" he asked.

"Nothing," she said too quickly. Indeed, what was up with her?

He deposited her on the bed, and then strode out of the room, calling over his shoulder, "Call me if you need me."

"Hey, Mason," she said, causing him to pause in the doorway.

"Throw away the monitor."

He only grinned cheekily, and disappeared through the open door. When he returned, knocking lightly on the now-closed door, he entered to find that Millie had already helped her get ready for the day. Her hair was washed and she was dressed in slacks and a light-knit sweater.

"Ready for breakfast?" he asked, bending to lift her and carry her to the recliner.

"You have a doctor's appointment today, don't you?" Millie directed to Lacey.

"I do, at two thirty. Mason is going with me."

"That was great news," Mason said, beaming. He lifted Lacey into the truck, once again assuring she was situated comfortably and safely.

"Yes. It's great to hear my leg is healing nicely," she said when he climbed into the driver's seat. He draped a protective arm around her and then squeezed lightly.

"You heard the doctor, right? No moving the leg for two more weeks and then . . ."

"And then I should be able to walk with crutches." She grinned excitedly, turning in the seat to meet his gaze. "Mason, thanks for everything. I know if you hadn't been there for me, my leg might not be in such good shape."

He didn't immediately respond, but instead watched her face. They were so close, only inches apart, that she could see the golden flecks in his eyes, just as he could see into the blue depths of hers. When he reached his hand toward her and ran a gentle finger across her lashes, almost of its own volition, her hand came up to rest on his face—a face so familiar, yet unfamiliar at the same time.

She stared in fascination at his eyes, the straight nose over full, masculine lips. Yes, Mason, but not the boy from her youth. Her expression was thoughtful, somewhat serious, whereas he watched her with a sparkle of humor in his eyes and the corners of his lips twitching into a smile. When he closed the distance between them, bringing their lips together in a lingering kiss, he was still smiling when he finally pulled back. An awed, answering smile came to her lips as she raised a tentative hand to her mouth. "Wow," she said.

"Wow," he echoed.

When they arrived back at his house, Millie greeted them at the door. "You have a guest," she told Lacey.

Mason, who was carrying her into the house before he retrieved her wheelchair, glanced around curiously. "I didn't see any car."

"Oh, he wasn't sure which house was yours and parked down the street," she informed them.

Inside the family room, they found Keith Dunne waiting. He rose when Mason strode in carrying Lacey.

After Mason put her down in the recliner, Keith hurried across the room to kiss her on the cheek. He took her hand and then stepped back to assess the leg. He grimaced painfully. "Ah, Lacey, that looks awful."

"I'm doing better," she assured him, and then turned to Mason. "This is Keith, my former boss."

He accepted Keith's outstretched hand, but she saw the hard set of his jaw. Although Mason smiled politely, she noticed the smile didn't quite reach his eyes.

"I'll be outside so you two can visit," he said, and then strode off.

She watched after him, wondering why he had departed so hastily. She didn't have time to ponder why, since Keith surprised her by dropping into the nearby loveseat.

"Lacey, good news," he enthused. "Jefferson announced he's retiring at the end of the month, so . . ." His eyes were alight with excitement. "So," he continued with relish, "Patrick, Dylan, and I would like you to take his place."

She shook her head, puzzled. "Wait, Keith, you had already offered to make me a partner. I'm confused. Did my getting the position hinge on Jefferson retiring?"

He winced. "Look, Lacey, you caught me. I offered you a partnership when there wasn't one to be had, but I was hedging my bets. I figured . . ." His words trailed off when he saw the stricken look on her face.

She wasn't sure what to say. This was her life they were talking about. She realized Keith was being awfully cavalier when it came to her livelihood. What if she had accepted the position—the position that wasn't—and then Jefferson had postponed his retirement? She would have returned to a job that wasn't actually open. What would she have done then? She would have been stranded and looking for work.

"How could you do that, Keith?" Lacey asked, struggling to keep the anger from her voice. "What if Jefferson hadn't retired?"

"Okay, you're right, I know what you're saying. But Lacey,

things are working out great. That's why I'm here." He shot a glance at her leg. "Okay, look, how long until you're out of that contraption?"

"It's going to be a while longer," she said. "Possibly quite a while longer."

"But will you be able to use crutches soon?" he asked eagerly.

"Hopefully within two weeks," she told him.

"That's great! There's just over two weeks until the end of the month. Jefferson goes out, and you come in."

"It's not that simple, Keith," she said in a weary tone. "I don't have a place to stay. Even if I'm using crutches, getting around is going to be difficult."

"You can stay with me," he said eagerly, "and we'll make every possible accommodation for you at the firm." He took his voice down a notch, almost pleading. "Look, Lacey, this is the opportunity of a lifetime. It's everything you've worked so hard for."

She couldn't deny it. A partnership in the firm had been her dream. But strangely, curiously, the dream wasn't a clear picture in her mind, but instead, a fuzzy rendition of what it had once been. What did she want? Did she want her old life back? Did she want out of Westover once and for all? And could she find the answers she was seeking regarding her parents if she were to return to Portland?

"Keith, I need time to think."

He was about to argue, but could tell by the set of her mouth that it wouldn't do him any good to push. He knew she couldn't be forced into anything. How often he had tried to counsel her as to which direction to take in some of her difficult cases. She had systematically rejected his suggestions, instead relying on her own instincts and experience in order to make what she deemed to be the best decisions for her clients. He couldn't deny she had good instincts, and he sincerely hoped those same instincts would lead her back to Portland.

He rose. "Look, call me. Soon." He brushed a kiss across her cheek. "You look good. Despite everything, you look good."

Millie showed Keith out, and Lacey felt her body go weak in the chair. A part of her wished he hadn't shown up. It wasn't necessarily that she didn't want what he offered, but she just didn't know for sure anymore.

Maybe she was just tired. Maybe, after a good deal of thought, she would know what to do. For now, she closed her eyes and went to sleep.

Later, Mason's deep voice penetrated her dream state. "She was up half the night watching a horror movie," he said.

"But she hates horror movies!" Lacey heard Robert declare. "Son, why would you let her watch a horror movie? You know what happened the last time she watched one."

Lacey opened her eyes, fixing a stare on Robert. "Pop, I was seven," she said, enunciating carefully. "Stop treating me as if I were still a child."

"Oh, honey," he said with a sigh, "you know I didn't mean anything by that. I just know that you have never, ever been able to watch a horror movie without experiencing nightmares for months on end. What's changed?"

"I was a child," she said. "*I've* changed."

"We'll see . . . ," he mused thoughtfully.

"So you know, Lacey," Mason piped in, smiling ruefully, "it looked like you were having a nightmare just then."

She pondered that for a moment. "Really?" Her eyes widened. "Yes, I guess I was."

"She'll need a night-light," Robert said succinctly.

"That's what I said," Mason said.

"Oh, brother," Lacey said.

Robert patted her on the head, much like he had done when she was a child. She didn't bother protesting. It wouldn't have done her any good.

"So, what's new with you, Pop?" she asked, casting aside her frustration with him. On some level, she understood it was difficult for him to see her as anything but the little girl she had been when he had known her years before. When she left town to attend college, he had still viewed her as a child, and in truth, she had been little more than a kid. That time seemed light-years behind her, she realized, but apparently not as long ago for him. She was lost to her thoughts, and hadn't noticed that Robert watched her with a self-satisfied gleam in his eye. When she did, she asked, "What, Pop?"

"I have a proposition to make, Lacey Jane," he said, almost smugly.

"What's that?" she asked, glancing at Mason, who shrugged.

"I've been thinking . . ."

"Oh, yeah? What about?"

"We need a lawyer in this town," he declared. "Now, Lacey," he said when she opened her mouth to speak, "hear me out. Yes, we're a small town here, but that's okay, because . . ." He fixed her with a look. "Aren't you going to ask me 'Because why?' "

"Because why?" she said obligingly, stifling a yawn.

"Because you'll be the only lawyer in town. Think of all the business you'll drum up."

"I don't know, Pop," she said, shifting in the chair. "I may be going back to Portland."

Mason glanced at her sharply. "You might?"

"Keith offered me a partnership," she told him.

He shook his head confusedly. "I thought he'd already offered you a partnership," he said, eyeing her questioningly.

"Well, yeah, but . . ." She waved off the explanation. "Anyway, he's asked me to return to Portland in two weeks, and then start back with the firm."

"You're going to be laid up much longer than two weeks," Mason pointed out.

"Dr. Marks said if all goes well, I can start using crutches in two weeks," she reminded him.

"He said you could use them, but slowly at first. Certainly not all the time. If you'll remember, he warned you about the consequences of doing too much too soon," he said, his voice suddenly monotone. "Lacey, you're not thinking straight."

"What? I'm thinking perfectly straight. I have a life, Mason. A life I may want to go back to—a life I probably should get back to sooner rather than later."

"Look," he said in an attempt at a placating tone, "be reasonable."

"Are you suggesting I'm not being reasonable?" she asked, taking a calming breath.

"Nobody's suggesting anything," Robert said.

"You are!" Lacey accused. "You're suggesting I open a law office in Westover, and *you!*" she said, pointing a finger at his son. "You're suggesting I'm not in my right mind, apparently."

"I'm suggesting no such thing," he said. "Of course you're in your right mind, but Lacey, your body is broken. If you start back to that job before your leg is ready, you could do irreparable damage to it. You know that." His voice was sincere, imploring.

She sighed heavily. He was right. What should she do? Should she risk her leg by returning to the hectic pace of the Portland firm? Could she even keep up the pace? Oh, why was life so complicated?

Mason read her silence as compliance. "Good," he murmured with relief. "Good."

Chapter Fifteen

"Mason, you should go out tonight," Lacey suggested. "Your friend Travis called again and asked if you were going to play basketball tonight at the church. He said your team really needs you. You should go. You've been cooped up with me for weeks now."

"I'm not complaining," he said, lowering the newspaper that had been in front of his face. "Hey, have you come to any decisions?"

She sipped her coffee. "No, not yet. I should give Keith a call."

He gave her a pointed look. "Do you really think you're ready to return to your former life?"

She considered the question. "I know I can do anything I set my mind to."

"But at a cost," he said testily, and dropped the paper onto the tabletop. "I think I am going out."

"Good," she said. "What are you going to do?"

He gave her an assessing glance. "Is that any of your business?"

"Having lunch with your assistant today?" she asked snidely.

"How'd you know she asked me to lunch?"

"I heard the message. Gah!" she said. "Asking you to a 'work' lunch on a Saturday. Talk about obvious. Work lunch! Ha!"

She had punctuated the word *work* by doing air quotes with her fingers, prompting Mason to laugh. If he didn't know better, he'd think she was jealous of Melissa—not that she had anything to worry about. Since the day he'd overheard his assistant's unkind remarks about Lacey, he hadn't thought of her in quite the same way. He had believed she was hardworking, inordinately professional—and kind. Now he wondered about the latter.

In her position, she was privy to a good deal of sensitive information, and he wondered now if she was as trustworthy as he had originally thought. He decided to mull it over later.

"Tell Melissa hi for me," Lacey called out as he strode toward the front door.

"Give Keith my best," he called in return. "Not!" she heard him grumble.

Lacey chuckled, and also heard Mason laughing as the door closed behind him. She knew he realized like she did that they were both being childish and ridiculous. Neither was behaving like the adults they were. Certainly not like the professionals they were.

Besides, it was neither here nor there to her if he had a lunch date with his obnoxious assistant. What business was it of hers? If he was attracted to gossiping, doe-eyed brunets, then, well, he deserved what he got.

She forced the thought of him and his impending lunch date from her mind as she dialed Keith. She had promised to call him, to tell him her intentions regarding the partnership. He wasn't going to like what she had to say—that, as yet, she hadn't made any decisions.

"Lacey," Keith said eagerly. "I'm so glad you called. Hey, I need to know what your plans are. We'd like you to start ASAP."

"Keith, my leg just isn't up to snuff yet."

"But you're able to use crutches, right?"

"As of today," she told him, "but only occasionally. I'm supposed to gradually build up to continued use of the crutches."

"Lacey," he persisted, practically whining.

"Look, if I have to give you an answer here and now, then the answer is no. I have no other choice."

"No, no, listen, you have time. I'll . . . buy time. I'll talk to the partners and make it happen."

"Okay, but Keith, I'm still not sure what my future holds. . . ."

"I know," he sighed, "but remember, we're offering you everything you've always wanted."

"Mason," Lacey said mock-sweetly, "thank you for cutting your lunch date short and bringing me to my grandma's house again."

"It was the least I could do," he said distractedly, "since you've badgered me constantly for the past two weeks." He paused, frowning. "Wait, what did you say? Hey! Just so you know, I didn't have lunch with Melissa today." He shook his head to clear it. "By the way, how'd your phone call with Keith go?" he asked, watching her intently.

"He's going to try to hold my job longer, if the partners go for it."

"Hmm," he murmured. "Do you want them to hold your job?"

She shrugged. "Yeah, I guess so. Of course, I've been living the life of leisure around your place. Who knows if I can adjust to my former work schedule? It was grueling," she said seriously.

"Which is why you shouldn't go back," he said. "Look, Lacey, sometimes we have to make sacrifices when fate intervenes. Your leg is not going to heal properly if you don't do what the doctor tells you."

"I plan to do what the doctor tells me," she assured him.

"How? How are you going to fit in your physical therapy

appointments between meetings with clients? And how are you going to get to your appointments? Being on crutches doesn't negate the fact that you're going to be stuck in a cumbersome cast for several months. And," he added, raising his pointer finger, "you're going to have to have a minor surgery soon."

"What?" she asked. "Another surgery? I'm confused. I thought . . ."

Mason noted the stricken look in her eyes. "Don't panic," he said in a softer voice. "The doctor has to remove those pins soon, and he can't do it without—"

"Cutting my leg open again," she said shrilly, and then shook her head. "How is it that I managed to forget that detail?"

"You probably blocked it out," he said with a grimace. "I would have. Keep in mind, though, that there'll be a recuperative period after the procedure."

She slumped in the seat. She was feeling frustrated, fearing she was doomed to be the invalid Mason's administrative assistant had said she was. The thought of the other woman caused her to feel a twinge of jealousy.

"If you had any sense, you'd fire that assistant of yours," she said hotly, from out of nowhere.

He tossed his head back and laughed heartily. "Oh, yeah? Where did that just come from?"

"Yeah," she said, "she's probably selling state secrets, or whatever the equivalent would be in the town of Westover. I'd keep my eye on the petty cash if I were you."

He chuckled. "Lacey, you are not very nice."

"Well, neither is she."

Mason wasn't going to argue with her. Melissa had hurt her with her unkind words. "Let's go in," he said.

"Okay."

He raised a clarifying finger and gave her a pointed look.

"What?" she said tiredly.

"No stair climbing. And keep your eyes on the floor, so you don't fall."

She rolled her eyes. "No backflips, no leaping off the landing of the stairs, no jumping on the beds, yada, yada, yada," she intoned.

He watched her with chagrin. "What has gotten into you?"

She threw up her hands at the clear blue sky. "I want to walk! I want to run! I want to—"

"Okay, I get the drift," he said. "You'll be able to do those things soon enough."

"No, not soon enough," she said testily.

"There are plenty of things to keep you busy," he suggested.

"Like what?"

"Well, you've discovered the Horror Channel," he said brightly.

"Yeah," she said with a quick grin. "I love it. Who knew?"

"Who knew?"

"Okay, let's get out of the truck," she urged him.

"Let me help you," he said, but by the time he climbed out of his truck and rounded the front, she had already dropped onto the ground. She struggled to land on the good foot, but to her dismay, her good foot had apparently atrophied somewhat, since it buckled beneath her. If Mason hadn't charged forward to catch her, she'd have crumpled to the ground.

"Good grief," she said, stunned.

"That was close," he muttered as he scooped her into his arms. "Would you please not do that again?"

"Mason," she said in measured tones, "put me down. If I don't walk on the crutches, I'm not going to be able to. It seems my good leg needs the exercise."

He grudgingly lowered her legs to the ground, watching her intently for any sign she might topple over. Once he was convinced she wasn't going to fall on her face, he hurriedly retrieved the crutches from the bed of the truck.

She took them and hobbled toward her grandmother's house. "Look at me," she said. "I'm upright."

"And you have opposable thumbs too," he said with a chuckle.

"Which I can very easily shove into your eyes," she warned.

He raised a hand as if in surrender. "Sorry, sorry," he muttered mock-contritely.

When they reached the front entrance to the home, Lacey paused at the threshold. She turned to Mason and smiled. "Home," she said softly.

He reached out to squeeze her hand, and then found the key in his pocket. He opened the door and helped her inside.

She stepped into the room, noting immediately that the air was stale. She saw glittering flecks of dust in the slanting sunshine streaming in through the windows. She hobbled over to a large window near the front door and attempted to open it.

"Lacey, I'll get it," Mason said, eyeing her with frustration. "All you have to do is ask."

She stepped back to watch him, balancing on her crutches for several seconds. When he had managed to hoist the window open, she took a step back and nearly fell over her grandmother's coffee table. Once again, he lunged forward and caught her. His muscular arms enfolded her waist, and she could only gasp as she realized she had almost fallen again.

She heaved a sigh of relief. "Okay, thanks, Mason," she said. "You can let go now."

"I don't think so," he muttered. "I don't think it's a good idea for you to move around the house with those crutches. There are too many obstacles."

"But I have so much to do," she said.

"Well, you're not doing it today," he responded.

She attempted to pull away from him, but he held firm. When

he hauled her against him, she watched him dazedly. What was he doing? He stared into her face. A ghost of a smile touched his lips. Did he find her amusing? she wondered. He always watched her with that same indulgent smile. When he reached out to smooth her hair away from her brow, she felt a veritable electric shock course through her.

Where had that come from? She swallowed hard and attempted to pull away. She suspected she knew where this was going. He held firm, and to her surprise, pulled her even tighter against him. He embraced her for a long moment, and she found herself surrendering to his warmth. But finally, she pulled away.

"Mason, let go of me," she said.

His voice was warm and husky when he spoke. "I'm afraid to."

"Well, as nice as this is . . ."

He pulled back abruptly, but didn't release her. "So, you think this is nice?"

She gave an almost imperceptible nod. "Right up there with three scoops of ice cream with sprinkles on top," she said softly, and then conceded with a shrug, "maybe even better."

He gave a self-satisfied smile. "This is nice too," he said, his voice warm and husky before his lips descended over hers in a kiss that caused her pulse to race. Her good knee practically buckled again, and if he hadn't been holding her upright, she feared she would have fallen over. She envisioned herself, stiff-legged and postured like a tree falling in the forest. "Timber," she said softly, against his lips.

"What did you just say?" he asked, his eyes alight with humor.

"Oh, nothing," she said, and then leaned in and claimed his lips this time. Although she had started it, he deepened the kiss, until Lacey wasn't sure she could take it any longer. Her body seemed to go limp, and he apparently sensed her difficulty remaining upright, since he scooped her up and carried her to the couch. Once there, he settled her on his lap and kissed her again.

When the kiss ended, she sighed. "That was nice."

"Better than ice cream?"

She nodded briskly.

"Glad you liked it," he said. He cocked his head to the side. "Can I assume that your liking my kiss means you like me too?"

She smiled, tracing his jawline with her finger. "I don't go around kissing just anybody," she murmured, holding his gaze. She shook her head suddenly, conveying her own surprise at her actions.

"What?" he asked, nuzzling her face with his cheek.

She pulled away from him. "I don't go around kissing *anybody*," she observed with wide-eyed wonderment.

"Gosh, what do you think it means?" he asked in a teasing voice.

She shrugged and said bemusedly, "I guess you aren't as ugly as you used to be."

Chapter Sixteen

Okay, look, Lacey, I know you want to get everything done all at once, but it's just not possible," Mason said.

"Ever the voice of reason," she said glumly. She sat on a chair at her grandmother's kitchen table—a table at which she had eaten many a breakfast, lunch, and dinner. A feeling of nostalgia washed over her. It felt right to be home, yet so wrong. Rennie wasn't here.

Mason sensed that she was on the brink of crying. He pulled up a chair next to her. "Hey, really, you've done a lot today. I think it's time you took a break."

"I haven't done much," she said, trying not to sniffle or break down.

"You've gone through piles of photos and organized them," he said. "That's enough for today."

"It's about the only job I can do in this cast," she said with frustration, and then glanced around. "There's so much more to do."

"I'll help you with everything," he promised.

"You have a life to get back to," she said, her shoulders drooping.

"What are you talking about? You are my . . ."

The words hung in the air. She watched him expectantly. Had he almost said what she thought he had? No. He had purposely refrained from finishing his thought. Surely that was significant.

She looked down at the box of photos in front of her. "There are so many," she said, attempting to change the subject. An awkward silence ensued. She glanced up tentatively and saw an array of emotions crisscross Mason's face. She couldn't read him and wanted to ask him what he was thinking. For reasons she couldn't fathom, she decided to leave it alone.

She glanced down at her hands, which were robotically thumbing through a stack of pictures. Her eyes lit on an unfamiliar face in one of the photos. "Hey," she said, swiping at her moist eyes, "who is this, Mason?"

"Who?" he asked, taking the photo. He studied it, recognizing his father as a young man. Another young man stood beside him. He resembled Robert, but whereas Robert had dark hair, this man's hair was bright blond, like . . .

"Who is he?" she asked, her voice barely above a whisper.

"I . . . don't know," he answered, turning the photo over. "It says here it's Dad and . . . Oh, okay, yeah. This is his older brother, Timothy."

"Mason, look at him."

He looked at the photo again and shrugged.

"Who does he look like?" she asked, her voice tight with anticipation.

He shrugged again.

"Mason, look at his hair!"

He looked at the young man's hair, and then he raised his bent head ever so slowly, his eyes lighting on Lacey's platinum-blond hair. He opened his mouth to speak, but promptly clamped it shut.

"Could he be . . . ?" she said, letting the words hang in the air.

He straightened in the chair. "I don't know, Lacey. I really don't know." Suddenly, his eyes widened and he looked like a deer caught in headlights.

"What?" Lacey cried.

"Ah, heck, did I just kiss my cousin?"

She watched him, stricken, but then remembered a very important detail. "Mason, you're adopted."

"Oh, thank god," he murmured. "Thank god."

Suddenly, his cell phone trilled in his shirt pocket. He snatched it out, checked the screen, and then flipped it open. "Yeah, Melissa, what is it?"

He listened intently, and then flipped the phone closed. Before he could speak, Lacey asked, "What's she doing working on a Saturday?"

"Trying to impress her boss," he said matter-of-factly. "Anyway, she called to tell me she just discovered a fax that came over from the college late yesterday."

Lacey gasped. "What did it say?"

"Let's go find out," he said.

At the station, Lacey relented and allowed Mason to push her inside in the wheelchair. He feared that navigating the maze-like hallways might be too much for her leg, considering she'd just begun using the crutches and had had several mishaps already.

She waited in his office while he went to talk to Melissa. He soon returned with several sheets of paper. He sat at his desk and began to read through the pile.

"What does it say?" Lacey asked eagerly.

"Give me a second," he said.

"Hurry," she said.

"I will."

She waited with bated breath, until he glanced up from reading. He smiled. "Okay, Lacey, according to these documents, which are copies of several college forms, your mother entered college as Jessie Karr . . . and left as Jessie Sanders."

Lacey's eyes widened in surprise. "She did get married during college then," she said.

He nodded. "She married another student. Okay, one other thing. Apparently your mom actually left during her *freshman* year, about the time of her name change."

Lacey emitted the long breath she'd been holding. "So she dropped out of school early, apparently to get married," she said, and then her eyes widened as understanding dawned. "She didn't want Grandma to know. She probably thought it would break Rennie's heart."

"Would it have?"

She pondered the question. "There's no disputing Grandma would have been disappointed, but she would never have turned her back on her child. You know Grandma; she made the best of every situation." She smiled at the thought, and then asked, "Is there anything else you can discern from the paperwork?"

He passed the sheets to her, and she scanned them quickly with a lawyer's critical eye. "Mason, look here. My father's name was Thomas Sanders, and did you see this?"

"What?" he asked, rising from his desk and coming to stand beside her. He draped an arm around her shoulder, and she instinctively leaned into it for support. He squinted to read the tiny writing she showed him.

"Look, doesn't this mean my father was involved in ROTC?"

He bent even closer to study the almost indiscernible writing. "I think you're right. Yes, I definitely see the letters R-O-T-C."

Lacey sighed heavily, taking the first proper breath since she'd arrived at the station. "Well, we have a name," she said gratefully. "Now I can start looking."

"I already have."

The voice came from the doorway. Lacey glanced up. Melissa

stood just back from the threshold, as if afraid to cross. Her eyes appeared sad, almost fearful.

"What is it, Melissa?" Mason asked.

"May I have a word alone with Lacey, please?"

He glanced at Lacey. She nodded.

Melissa stepped into the room after Mason had left. "Look," she began, averting her eyes for several seconds before forcing herself to make eye contact again. "I wanted to apologize for that day, here at the department. I know you overheard the things I said, and I . . ."

She took a deep, shoring breath. "My behavior was inexcusable, and I've thought a lot about it over the past couple of weeks."

Lacey didn't speak, and Melissa apparently took her silence as a cue to continue. "I guess I was talking about your . . . well, background, in order to deflect from my own past—to try to elevate myself in some way." She wrung her hands nervously. "Here's the thing. I come from a pretty rough background. We didn't have much. And . . . my folks certainly had skeletons in their closets. My whole life, I bore the burden of their mistakes. It took me years before I could hold my head up high," she said shakily. "In light of that reality, I don't know what possessed me to be so cruel to you. I really don't know." Her voice faltered and she paused to search Lacey's face. "Will you forgive me for my behavior? I am sorry." She watched her with imploring eyes. "Can we start over?"

Lacey searched the other woman's face this time. Her brown eyes appeared sincere, and she felt her contrition was genuine. She extended a hand to her. "I'm Lacey," she said.

She heaved a sigh of relief. "I'm Melissa. Pleased to meet you."

As Lacey and Mason drove to the small town of Woodville, two hundred miles north of Westover, in hopes of obtaining additional information about her father, her mind drifted from one thought to the next. She remembered Melissa's apology. She wondered, had Melissa had experiences growing up in Westover similar to her own? Had she let her experiences color her thoughts about her hometown and the people in it?

She had remained in Westover, despite an apparent difficult background, whereas Lacey had hightailed it out of town as fast as her legs would take her. And now, she couldn't hightail it anywhere, since neither one of her legs was working particularly well. She was still surprised at how weak even her unbroken leg felt.

Her thoughts also turned to the picture she had found in Rennie's photo box. She had truly thought the young man, with hair so similar to her own, might be her father, but it turned out he could not have been. According to Robert, who Mason had called on their way to the station earlier, his brother Timothy had died as a young man of nineteen, well before she was born.

It appeared Thomas Sanders was indeed her father. She hoped desperately to learn more about him once she and Mason arrived at Woodville. Unfortunately, they had little to go on, other than a name and an address. She didn't hold out much hope about the address. It was rare for people to remain in their homes as long as Rennie had, or Robert's parents.

As Lacey sat beside Mason in the truck, her back against him and her leg jutting out in front of her, she wondered about both her mother and father. Had her mother refrained from mentioning her marriage and baby to Rennie because she couldn't bear to disappoint her? If so, her mother had sorely misjudged her own mother. But then, she had to concede that she would have rather died herself than disappoint Rennie.

And if Jessie had become pregnant with Lacey *before* marrying Thomas, then maybe she just couldn't bear to break that news to her mother. Rennie had had a staunch moral compass and might have been upset. But she also knew in her heart that her grandmother would have rallied. It was simply her nature to be loving and kind. She wondered, had Jessie inherited her mother's sweet temperament?

And her father . . . What kind of a man was he? Had he known about her? She couldn't discern from the papers the college had faxed over whether or not Jessie and Thomas had remained together. College records showed they had moved off campus, and then, of course, her mother had dropped out of school. Thomas had graduated, having earned his degree the winter of the year Jessie had shown up at Rennie's house. But as to whether or not they were still together at that point, who knew?

Her eyes widened. Her parents' off-campus address might be a lead she and Mason could follow. Perhaps there were people in the neighborhood who remembered the young couple, but she didn't hold much hope of that. If the two had resided in an apartment, which was likely, then anyone who might have known them had probably long since moved away.

She sighed, and Mason reached for her hand, giving it an encouraging squeeze. She held it as if holding on for dear life.

"Talk to me," he urged.

She sighed. "I'm just nervous. I feel like we're close, Mason."

She had said *we're* close, and it warmed his heart.

"I feel like we're close too," he said.

"Mason, what are we going to do once we get to Woodville? We can't very well get a phone book and start calling each and every Sanders in the white pages."

"Well, we could," he said, "but we'd be better off stopping by the local police station and inquiring there."

"Will they help us, do you think?"

He smiled. "Sure they will. I know several officers there. Good men," he said. "We've worked together on a case or two."

She nodded, satisfied. She was silent for a couple moments, but then turned slightly in the seat to see his face. "Mason, have you given any thought to trying to locate your biological parents?"

He glanced at her briefly and shrugged. "To be honest, not really. If somebody shows up, asking about me, I won't turn them away. But I've had a good life with Dad, and of course, Rennie, and . . . you."

She smiled. They had been a family. When Lacey's grandfather had passed, and then Robert's mother and father in close succession years later, Rennie had become a surrogate mother to the adult child of her best friend, just as Robert had been a surrogate father to Rennie's granddaughter. Lacey acknowledged that families came in many forms.

She also realized that Mason had been a fixture in her life, a cousin, protector, and able competitor. She'd certainly seen him as many things, but lately, she'd been seeing him through entirely different eyes.

"I don't find anyone by that name," the officer said, wincing apologetically. "We have several people named Sanders in town, and I suppose any one could be related to this Thomas Sanders, but I find no record of him."

"I guess we'll have to start calling phone numbers out of the book," Mason said, and then thanked the officer for his help. He pushed Lacey in her wheelchair back to his truck.

"I wish we had some way of knowing if Thomas had any relatives in town," she said.

"Wait," he said, "I'm going to call Melissa and have her place a call to the college and find out if they have any other information to give us."

"Don't colleges require an emergency contact number or the name of a family member on certain forms?"

Mason mulled over the question. "You're right." He quickly called Melissa, asking her to check with the college about any emergency contact number or names of relatives on a contact list.

"Why don't we grab lunch and wait for Melissa to return the call," he suggested.

Inside the restaurant, he asked, "If you don't mind my asking, what did Melissa have to say to you back at the station?"

"She apologized for the things she said."

He weighed the information with a nod. "Really? That was . . ."

"Brave of her," Lacey supplied.

"So . . . you . . . accepted her apology?" he asked, curious.

"I did," she told him.

"You did?"

"Why does that surprise you? I'm not a child. I don't hold grudges."

"Well, except against the town as a whole," he said matter-of-factly, and then bit into his hamburger.

She glared at him, unsure how to respond. What did he know about it? How could he possibly understand how she felt? He'd grown up the son of one of the town's wealthiest families. He had no idea what she had gone through as a child, finding herself the brunt of speculation and unkind talk at every turn. It . . . hurt.

Mason could see he'd angered her. He reached a hand across the table, attempting to take her hand in his own. She pulled away.

"I'm sorry," he said. "I understand where you're coming from."

"You couldn't possibly. You grew up in a wealthy home and never wanted for anything. People didn't whisper about you when you walked past them."

"Sure they did," he said. "I was the 'adoptive' son of the wealthiest family in town."

"No, you were adopted into the 'right' family. Nobody talked about the James family. It was almost sacrilege to talk about the mighty Jameses."

"Oh, people talked about us, all right," he said. "Of course, you never heard it because you were too busy listening for your own name."

"Mason, that's not fair!" she cried. "I was a little kid, and you *know* the things people said about me."

"Yes, and it was inexcusable that you were subjected to it, but Lacey, you're a grown woman now. Back then, you had us to protect you. And we did. Dad, Rennie, and I. Even Donna. It's time to let go of the past, to let bygones be bygones and live your life."

"You mean, live my life in Westover."

"Yes," he said succinctly, holding her gaze for long seconds.

She opened her mouth to speak, but promptly clamped it shut. She'd almost said, when hell freezes over. But how often in her life had she said she wouldn't give Mason James the time of day until pigs flew?

She nearly groaned aloud. Well, apparently swine had taken to the sky, because she wanted to give him much more than the time of day. So much more.

Chapter Seventeen

After finishing their lunch in silence, Mason borrowed a phone book from the fast food restaurant and set about listing all the names and numbers of the town's Sanderses.

Thankfully, there were only seventeen, which seemed a daunting enough number.

Suddenly, his cell phone rang. "Yeah, Melissa. What have you got?" he asked. He listened, unspeaking, said, "Thanks," and then hung up.

"What'd she say?" Lacey asked.

"Since it's Saturday, she couldn't manage to get ahold of anybody at the college." He gave a self-deprecating laugh. "Should have figured that out for ourselves. Anyway, she did fax over a request for additional information, including any names of relatives, as well as contact numbers or any addresses."

Lacey nodded, and then turned her attention back to the list of names in front of her. "I'm going to start calling," she declared, and did just that.

She'd run through half the list, but hadn't found anyone who knew a Thomas Sanders. "This is frustrating," she said, smoothing her hand through her hair.

"Give me part of the list."

She tore the bottom portion of the sheet, giving Mason a short list to call.

"Nothing," he said finally.

"Nothing," she echoed.

He checked his watch. "We'd better go. We have a long drive ahead of us."

"I hate to leave," she told him as he pushed her wheelchair toward the truck. "I feel like we're close."

"I know. Hey, Lacey Jane . . ."

"Yeah?"

"I'm sorry about— Well, you know."

She knew he was apologizing for their tiff in the restaurant. "Yes, I know."

"We're not giving up," he said.

"I know."

"Hopefully, we'll have something Monday, once the college receives our request for information."

"Hopefully," she mused. "Hopefully."

They drove home in relative silence, each lost to their respective thoughts. Lacey couldn't stop thinking about her father. Thomas Sanders. She was actually Lacey Sanders.

She suddenly felt deflated, however, when she realized that was sheer speculation. For all she knew, this Sanders fellow wasn't even her father. She didn't know her mother. She certainly had no memories of her, since she had left her behind when she was barely two years old. Maybe Jessie wasn't the sweet girl Robert and Millie had purported her to be. Maybe she had changed.

It happened. Young people went off to college, engaged in experimental behaviors, and soon became entrenched in things that weren't particularly good for them. While many came out the other side, perhaps unscathed—or not—they managed to learn from their experiences and go on to lead productive lives. Many didn't. Was that the case with her mother? Had she become involved in things she shouldn't have? Maybe . . . she had *meant* to leave her behind.

She also wondered, had Thomas Sanders been a good man?

And what if her mother had left him and been involved with someone else after? If that turned out to be the case, her search would come to a dead end. She sincerely hoped her mother had remained married to Thomas Sanders, that he was a good man, and that there was a logical explanation as to why he had never come to get her after her mother's death.

When they arrived back home late, they found Robert waiting on the front porch.

"Why didn't you use your key, Pop?" Mason asked.

"Forgot it," he said. "So, any luck?" he asked, glancing from his son to Lacey.

She shook her head. "No luck. According to the paperwork the college faxed over, my mother married a man named Thomas Sanders. And it turns out she actually quit school during her freshman year."

"Really?" Robert mused.

The trio went into the house, Mason pushing Lacey's wheelchair. She was too drained both emotionally and physically to use the crutches.

"Okay," Robert clarified, "so she dropped out of school her freshman year and became pregnant. That's pretty much what we'd figured, isn't it?"

Lacey nodded, eyeing the comfort of Mason's overstuffed recliner.

"And Jessie was married," Robert said, a slight smile curving his mouth. "I figured as much."

"You did?" Lacey said.

"I told you, your mama was a good girl. Not that—" He raised a finger to emphasize his point. "Not that she wouldn't still be a good girl had she gotten pregnant out of wedlock. Frankly, it happens all the time to perfectly sweet, decent, hardworking kids. People are human," he said succinctly. "They make mistakes. It's part of the job description." Robert paused, but then pinned her with his gaze. "Take you, for example, Lacey."

Her eyes widened. "What did I do?" she griped. She shot a longing look at the recliner, and Mason noticed this time. He lifted her and deposited her onto the chair with nary a word.

"As I was saying . . . ," Robert said. "Take you, for instance, Lacey. You've made huge mistakes."

"I have?"

"Yes," he said with a nod of his head. "You hold grudges."

She shot him a dirty look. His son had told her the very same thing earlier. Robert ignored her scathing glance. "Now, don't feel bad. I have my own flaws."

"Really?" she said sarcastically. "Do tell."

Robert ignored the question. "Even Mason has made mistakes," he acknowledged.

"Such as?" Mason asked, crossing the room and sitting down on the couch. "Fill me in, Pop."

She heard the sarcastic note in Mason's voice, but if Robert did, he didn't let on.

"Don't mind if I do," he said obligingly, and turned to Lacey. "My son has this problem, you see. He just can't seem to express himself when he really needs to."

"I express myself just fine, thank you very much," Mason grumbled, and then picked up the remote and turned on the television.

The Horror Channel came on, and Lacey turned toward it, eager to see what was playing. Robert noticed and wagged a warning finger. "You'll have nightmares."

"I'm a grown woman," she said in a singsong voice.

"You'll have nightmares," Mason said, and switched the channel.

"Son, I was talking to you," Robert said pointedly.

"Oh, yeah? Why don't we go back to talking about her?"

"I'll talk *to* Lacey then," Robert said agreeably. "As I was saying, Mason can't express himself to save his life when it comes to talking about emotions. Oh, sure, he can communicate on the job, and he can even keep up a witty repartee when he feels like it, but when it comes to expressing real, honest-to-goodness emotion, he just won't do it."

"Not true," Mason said in a monotone voice.

"Oh?" Robert raised an eyebrow and watched his son with a challenging glint in his eye. "Well, here's an example. Let's say you, son, had feelings for a woman. Now, we're not talking about any particular woman, and keep in mind this is just for the sake of argument. But let's say you have feelings for a woman, Mason, strong feelings, even. Do you tell her?"

Mason ignored the question, and instead turned the television back to the Horror Channel. "Look, Lacey, it's a repeat of the movie from the other night."

"Mason is deflecting," Robert said, catching Lacey's eyes. "He's good at it."

"Dad, would you stop watching those shrinks on TV?" Mason grumbled.

Lacey couldn't help but look at the television screen. Her eyes were drawn to the horror playing out there. That house was pulsing again.

Robert watched the television briefly, and then made a face. "Well, they do say that home is where the heart is," he said wryly. "And that takes me right back to what I was talking about, Mason."

He gave his father a confused glance. "What?" he said, laughing lightly.

"As I was saying—"

"You were just saying you were leaving, Pop," Mason said, rising from the couch. "It's late and you need your sleep."

"I'm fine," Robert assured his son.

"Lacey is tired. She really needs her rest."

He knew Robert wasn't about to argue with that. It was late, and Lacey did need her rest. Robert rose slowly from the love-seat. "We'll have to pick up this conversation later."

"Or not," Mason said drolly.

After Robert had left, Lacey turned to Mason briefly. "What was all that about?"

He couldn't believe his good fortune. Had she really not understood the meaning of his father's banter? If not, he'd made a lucky escape. The Horror Channel had served a purpose, after all.

"Are you ready for bed?" he asked.

She glanced his way, but promptly turned back to the television screen. "I'm going to watch this movie again."

"Why?" he asked.

She shrugged without looking at him. "I don't know. I guess I'm hooked on this network."

"Well, good night, then," he said.

"Oh, you're leaving?" She frowned worriedly at the prospect. "Do you want me to stay?"

She nodded, without taking her eyes from the screen.

"Good grief, Lacey, I can see your brain rotting as we speak."

"What?"

"Nothing."

When the movie ended and the credits rolled down the screen, she turned to Mason, who appeared to be sleeping. She noted the rise and fall of his broad chest. Just to be sure he was out, she said softly, "So you have trouble expressing yourself, eh?"

Robert and Mason were right. Lacey had nightmares. Like a video, they had replayed over and over in her mind. By morning, she woke up feeling as if she'd just run a marathon—through a house with pulsating walls.

Mason rose from the couch and stretched, eyeing her ruefully as he took in the dark half-circles that framed her lower lids. "Are we giving up horror movies?" he asked sweetly.

"I think so," she said, yawning.

"Do you know how to unblock a channel?" he asked.

When she gave him a puzzled glance, he surmised she didn't. He knew it was for the best he make the Horror Channel inaccessible, since she would probably be sucked back in soon enough. Of course, if he told her his intent, she'd be furious—and probably rightly so. But lately, she often seemed to need saving from herself. He also realized she was in dire need of mental stimulation.

"Hey, after Millie gets here and helps you get ready, why don't I set you up in front of the computer and you can start a search for the Sanders name?"

"Mason, why are you talking to me as if I were a small child?"

"I'm not," he said. "I'm talking to you as if you're an adult whose mind has been taken over by the Horror Channel."

She eyed him thoughtfully. "Okay."

"Okay?" he said. "Is this a trick?"

"Why would you ask me that?"

"Since when do you give in so easily? Shouldn't you be ranting and raving about how you're an adult and how I have no business telling you what you can or can't watch on television?"

"I'm a guest in your home. Of course I'll conduct myself in accordance with your rules."

"I don't have any rules. And you are not a guest."

"Yes, I am."

"No, you're not." He raked a hand through his hair. "I need a shower. And I'm done sleeping on that couch, by the way. We both have perfectly good beds to sleep in. You'll be back in yours tonight," he said.

Lacey bit back a retort. He was right. She'd awakened weary and with a crook in her neck. It only made sense that she return to the comfort of the bed, where she could sprawl out.

And he needed his rest. As the sheriff of Westover, he needed his sleep to assure he was alert and at the ready while doing his job. Lack of sleep slowed the reflexes, and her recent love affair with horror flicks had likely had the unwanted effect of slowing Mason's. In truth, it hadn't done much for hers, either.

"Lacey, I have to get to work." Mason glanced at his watch. "Look, I hate to leave you, since Millie isn't here yet. Will you be okay until she gets here?"

These days, Millie wasn't coming as early as she had been, since Lacey could manage fairly well on her crutches. Mason insisted, though, that she continue coming for part of the day should Lacey need anything. She half suspected he worried that she'd be lonely.

"I'll be just fine," she told him from her place at the computer in his home office.

"Any luck?" he asked.

She sighed. "No, nothing. Do you know how many guys named Thomas Sanders there are in this world?"

He shrugged. "There can't be too many who attended Tate College, or who married Jessie, or who apparently lived in Woodville."

She rolled her shoulders in an attempt to get the kinks out of her neck. She'd spent many hours at the computer the evening before, and had taken up residence in the chair bright and early this morning.

Mason crossed the room and began to massage her shoulders. She melted against him, succumbing to the pleasure of his strong hands. "Mmm, that feels good," she said.

"Maybe you should take a break," he suggested. "You feel all knotted up."

She turned toward him. "I am all knotted up."

He pulled back. "I wish I didn't have to leave right now."

"I'll see you when you get home tonight."

"I'll stop by at lunchtime," he said.

"You have a lunch meeting."

"I do?" He furrowed his brow. "With who?"

"With a Sergeant Price," she told him, tapping the desktop calendar.

He laughed. "Well, thanks for the heads-up," he told her, smiling into her eyes. "Anything else I need to know?"

"We need bread."

He chuckled. "We've become like an old married couple."

"Who are you calling old?" she asked, without skipping a beat or looking at him.

"Not you!" he said, raising his hands in surrender. He gave her a chaste kiss on the cheek and then sauntered out of the room.

"Yeah, well, that was definitely an old married couple kind of kiss," she mumbled, unaware he had heard her.

He strode back into the room, a wide grin spanning his face. "You want a *real* kiss?"

"Didn't say that," she muttered.

"You implied it."

"I did?" She turned to him this time, her smile matching his now. When he leaned in and claimed her lips, she responded to his kiss. When they finally parted, his eyes held a small glow of satisfaction as he spun on his heel and walked out of the room.

"Watch the leg!" he called, and then she heard the front door close behind him.

Lacey experienced an odd feeling of abandonment. Could

she possibly miss him when he'd been gone all of thirty seconds? What was happening to her? She'd just kissed him! Again! And she had liked it! No, she had more than liked the kiss. She had craved his kiss. Good grief, she muttered. The world had suddenly gone topsy-turvy.

He was Mason James, for Pete's sake, the bane of her existence for so many years. Now . . .

In an attempt to get her mind off him and their kiss, she rose from the chair. She reached for her crutches and carefully hobbled into the family room. She cast a glance at the TV. Anything good on the Horror Channel? she wondered, but quickly cast the idea aside. She was fast becoming a couch potato and a television junkie. Until her injury, she had gone for months without having a look at prime time programming, let alone daytime TV.

She stood in the middle of the room, the crutches under her arms keeping her upright. She sighed loudly. She was bored. It was midweek, and had she been home in Portland and on the job, she might have been in court, directing potential jurors as to the difference between "preponderance of the evidence" and "beyond a reasonable doubt." She might have been conferring with the judge, or cross-examining a witness. The job had been challenging, fast-paced, and rewarding. She had loved it.

Suddenly, she felt bone-weary. She shot a glance at her leg. She'd taken to wearing Mason's sweatpants, so as to hide the contraption encasing her leg from onlookers. In truth, *she* didn't want to see it. She wondered how it would look when all the external hardware was removed and the rows of pins taken out. The mere thought of those pins, piercing her skin and anchored into the bone, caused a wave of nausea to wash over her.

Focusing on her injury was a time-waster, she promptly decided. She knew she couldn't change it, so she realized she would be better served if she didn't think about it. If she could ultimately regain full function of the leg, she knew she would be grateful.

When her cell phone rang, she carefully reached for it in one of the front pockets of her sweats. She teetered slightly from the action, but managed to remain upright. It was Keith on the other end.

"How are you?" he asked.

How was she? "Better, I think," she told him.

"Uh, Lacey, the partners are starting to press me for a date when you can start. They want to know, if you don't want the partnership, if you'll come back to your previous position."

"What?" she asked, confused. Why would they even think she might return to her prior job?

"Look, if you don't take the partnership, then Lon Miller has been slated for the position. If he ultimately takes it—if you're unable to, that is—then that opens up his position and will mean we need to hire another attorney to round out the firm."

"So you never intended to fill my spot?" she asked. "If I accept the partnership?"

"No. Like many other firms in town, we've fallen on hard economic times. We've had to tighten our belts. This too shall pass," he said encouragingly, "but that brings me to another point."

"And what is that?" she asked, running a hand through her hair. She knew the firm needed her answer, but she just didn't know what her future held.

"Have you given any thought to suing the kids who ran the light and hit you that night?"

Her eyes widened in shock. The thought hadn't even occurred to her. Her mind had been on Rennie, and then her own injury, and the fallout from that injury as far as her living arrangements went. "No, Keith, I haven't. I haven't even discussed the accident with Mason."

"It's time you did," he said.

She took a deep, shoring breath. "Look, I can't think about this now."

"What do you know about these kids?" Keith persisted.

"Nothing."

"Well, I did some digging and they come from prominent families in a town not far from Westover. One has had an MIP, and the other was picked up for two DUIs. The second kid hasn't faced any real consequences for his behavior, because, well, money talks."

Lacey digested the information. She hadn't even thought about legal action relating to the kids. She guessed she'd just assumed that local law enforcement, and the prosecutor's office, were handling things.

"Lacey, your leg may never be the same. Those kids need to pay."

"You mean their families need to pay," she said.

Keith was silent for a moment, but Lacey could hear him breathing. She could tell he was attempting to keep his voice cool and steady when he spoke. "Lacey, think about what I've told you. They should face some serious consequences for their actions. You're certainly facing some serious consequences for them."

She couldn't deny that. "Look, Keith, I need to think. About a lot of things. I'll get back to you."

"Don't be too long," he cautioned. "About the partnership or the possible lawsuit. Time is of the essence."

"Yes, time," she muttered.

Chapter Eighteen

Mason, have you heard anything from the college yet?" Lacey inquired over breakfast the next day.

He glanced up and shook his head. "No, but I did call them. It turns out they don't have ready access to old records. All their archives are stored in a basement somewhere, and it happens that much of the students' paperwork from our time frame is missing."

"Missing? How?"

He shrugged. "I don't know, but the admissions representative I talked to assured me they'll find what we need. They just need some time."

"But they were able to give us the other paperwork," she reminded him. "The ones with the information about my mother."

He nodded. "Now we're asking for records specific to Thomas Sanders, and apparently they've misplaced the boxes with records of names ending in 'N' through 'Z.' But don't worry. They'll find them."

"I hope so," she mused.

"Hey," he began tentatively, "have you made any decisions about your former workplace?"

"You mean, am I going to take the partnership?" She sighed. She just didn't know. Keith had thrown her for a loop when he'd explained his logic in offering her the position in the first place. What if Jefferson hadn't made the decision to retire? Offering a position to someone when the job opening wasn't a sure thing seemed duplicitous to her. She wondered why Keith was so determined that she return to Portland and to the firm.

She knew the answer. He had made no secret about the fact he was attracted to her.

She also wondered, however, if she could even trust there was a partnership role waiting for her at the firm. She smoothed a hand through her hair, a gesture Mason recognized as a nervous one.

"What's on your mind, Lacey Jane?" he asked, smiling.

She shrugged. "Just can't seem to make up my mind these days," she told him.

"What's the hurry?" he said with a neither-here-nor-there shrug. "It's not like you're in any shape to go traipsing off to Portland."

"Traipsing?" she said, eyeing him through narrowed eyes. "This is my future we're talking about, Mason."

He pinned her with a gaze. "I'm worried about the future of that leg," he said, nodding toward it. "If you don't listen to the doctor, there's no telling what kind of damage you could still do to it."

She gave him a frustrated glance. "I'm being careful," she said. "Am I not the embodiment of caution when it comes to this leg?"

He considered the question. "So far, but if you return to your job sooner than is medically prudent, there's no telling." He rose from the table and dropped his plate into the sink. He turned. "Done?" She nodded and he took her plate. "I have no doubt that if you return to that job before your leg is properly healed, you'll end up in worse shape. And," he said, raising a finger, "I know you. You'll forget all about your leg when your mind is on your work. Heck, you'll probably forgo physical therapy and—"

"Mason, give me some credit," she cut in. "I'm not going to mess up this leg any worse than it already is." She rose and hobbled into the office, where she promptly settled in behind the computer.

He followed. "Look, I didn't mean to upset you. I worry, okay?"

"You don't need to."

"Oh, yeah? Is that right?"

"That's right," she told him, turning away from the computer briefly. Her eyes lit on the desktop calendar. "Hey," she cried, "you have an out-of-town conference on Monday and . . ." She studied the calendar. "You'll be gone for the whole week."

"I'm not going."

"What?" she demanded. "Why?"

"Why do you think?"

Her shoulders sagged. "Because of me?"

He shrugged. "Well, yeah. I'm not leaving you alone."

"Mason," she said with a frustrated sigh, "I'm fine. What's this conference about, anyway?"

"It's no big deal," he told her, averting his eyes.

"It is too! You couldn't even look at me when you said that."

He turned and met her gaze. "It's no big deal," he repeated.

"Tell me, specifically, what does this conference pertain to?"

"Oh, I won an award, but it's—"

"No big deal," she cut in drolly. "What kind of an award?" she asked eagerly.

He shook his head. "I've been selected the state's law enforcement officer of the year."

"You were? That's great, Mason. You have to go!"

"No, I don't. They'll send me the plaque. No big deal."

"It *is* a big deal," she said firmly. "And you *are* going."

"What about you?"

"What about me?" she asked, puzzled.

"I'm just not comfortable leaving you, that's what."

"I'm a grown woman. I'm perfectly capable of taking care of myself." Her eyes widened as an idea formed. "Go to your conference. While you're gone, it'll be a good time for me to move into Grandma's place."

"What?" he demanded, shaking his head in puzzlement.

"What do you mean, 'what'? That's always been the plan."

"No, it hasn't. And how do you plan to make a move in your condition?"

"My condition?" Lacey let out a low, frustrated growl and then took a deep breath and counted to ten. "Look, I'm getting around fairly well with the crutches. It's time I got out of here and you got your life back."

"That's ridiculous. I have a life."

"Yeah, a life that is obviously revolving around me and my problems. Go to your conference."

She paused, suddenly remembering her conversation with Keith about the boy who had plowed his car into her. She frowned. "Mason, do you have any idea what's going on with the kid who hit me? From a legal standpoint?"

She saw his eyes harden and his lips compress. "The driver, at nineteen, is an adult, and is currently lodged in jail. The younger kid is home, but I've been in communication with his parents." He gave her an assessing glance. "Why do you ask?"

She shrugged. "Keith brought them up."

"Let me guess. He's thinking lawsuit."

She nodded. "He suggested it."

"What are you thinking?"

She shook her head. "To be honest, I don't want to go there. I'd like to think the boys will face consequences for drinking and driving. I have more pressing things to deal with right now."

"They could have killed you," Mason mused, running a hand through his hair. He seemed lost in thought for a moment. "Fortunately, the driver had insurance, and I've been in communication with his insurance company on a near-daily basis."

Lacey gasped. "You have not!" She slumped in the chair. "Oh, Mason, I'm sorry. I didn't realize. I should have been dealing with everything—fighting my own battles."

"You haven't been in any shape to deal with all this. And I don't mind doing it for you."

She met his gaze, and reached out to squeeze his hand. How much more could she expect from this man? He had practically given up his life for her. It just wasn't fair to him. There was no way he was going to miss that conference.

"You are going to that conference, Mason, and you're going to enjoy it. And when they present you with that award, you will smile for the camera, so I'll see proof that you were there!"

Mason eyed her, and she could see the wheels turning in his head. "If I go, will you stay here while I'm gone?"

"Mason . . ."

"Lacey, listen. I know you think I'm being heavy-handed, and I know you're tired of being here, but Rennie's house isn't ready for occupation as yet. There's a lot of deferred maintenance and I haven't had a chance to check it out."

"What kind of deferred maintenance?" she inquired. "And any deferred maintenance is my worry, not yours." She felt sick. On top of everything else, he felt responsible for the maintenance of *her* home. How much more could one man take?

"You need a break, Mason!" she charged. "Run, don't walk, to that conference!"

He bit back a frustrated growl this time, and then appeared to take a deep breath. "Look, about the house, there are loose boards on the steps and porch. There are several raised edges on the floors, which would be a real hazard where you're concerned. Rennie mentioned something about a roof leak. I don't know what else," he admitted, "but I'd feel better if you let me check it out before you move in. I would have done it already, but . . ."

"But you've been busy playing nursemaid to me," she said sadly. "Not to mention everything else you've done for me. Listen, I'll take care of everything. It's my responsibility."

He shook his head and folded his arms across his chest. She recognized the gestures. He wouldn't budge on this.

"Go to your conference," she commanded. "If you don't go, I *will* leave. I can't stand to think you'll miss something important to you—to your career—because of me."

"I'll go," he relented, "but only if you give me your word you won't make a move until I get back."

He was the most frustrating man. If she didn't make him that promise, she knew he wouldn't attend the conference. It would weigh on her conscience for the rest of her days if he missed that conference.

"All right," she said resignedly. "I'll stay here, but just until you get back."

"All right," he said, the relief evident in his voice.

"When do you leave?"

"Are you that eager to see me go?" he asked, watching her with unconcealed interest.

"It's not that . . ."

"Then what is it?"

"Nothing." She wasn't about to tell him that, in truth, she liked having him around. Maybe too much. She was settling into his home, and found herself getting a tad too comfortable. That realization was shocking to her. She'd lived alone since she'd left Westover for college. She'd been independent like Rennie, and couldn't abide the thought of having a roommate. But now . . .

When Mason was at work, she often found herself glancing at the clock. She missed him when he was gone and couldn't wait for him to come home. During the past several days, she hadn't thought much about her job, or the partnership.

She told herself it was because of her leg—that the leg precluded her from seriously considering going back to work in the near future. However, she well knew that the woman she'd been before would have moved mountains to achieve her goals. She wouldn't have let a broken leg stop her. Heck, she was on crutches now and had some mobility. Really, what was stopping her from returning to Portland today?

She sighed loudly and Mason cleared his throat. "Wow, where'd you just go?" he asked. "Now what's on your mind?"

She wasn't about to tell him. Absolutely not. She couldn't possibly tell him that he was the reason she was stalling about her job. What was happening to her?

She refrained from dropping her head onto folded arms. He would really wonder what was up with her then.

"Lacey . . . ," Mason intoned. "Earth to Lacey."

"I'm back," she told him with a long sigh.

He stuck out his hand. "We have a deal."

She nodded obligingly and took his hand. "Yeah, I'll stay here until you get back. I don't know why it's so important to you, but I'll stay."

Mason left for his conference early Monday morning, just after Millie arrived with a suitcase in hand. Although Lacey was pleased to see her, she felt awful that once again, Mason felt obliged to hire help for her.

As the week progressed, with him gone at his conference, Lacey felt herself going stir-crazy. She had cabin fever, despite the fact that Millie was a constant companion. By Wednesday afternoon, she felt the walls closing in on her. Millie had run to the store for groceries, and she was stretched out in the recliner, contemplating her future plans.

When the phone rang, she jumped, and then hoisted herself out of the chair. She glanced around, looking for the cordless phone. She realized she'd left it beside the computer in the home office, just off the kitchen.

She hurried toward the phone, but registered the answering machine click on before she could reach it. She realized she should have been more conscientious about keeping the phone close at hand.

Suddenly, her ears alerted when she heard Melissa's voice on the message being recorded. "Miss Karr, this is Melissa, with the sheriff's office. I wanted to let you know we've finally heard back from the college. . . ."

Lacey's eyes widened. She needed to get to that phone! Picking up the pace, she struggled to cross the carpeted room in order to reach the nearby office. Unfortunately, to her horror, one of the crutches hit the slick tile in the kitchen, causing her to trip and launch face first through the open office door. A shriek of pain escaped her lips when her broken leg struck the doorframe.

Millie had just walked into the kitchen with a bag of groceries and had witnessed her tumble through the doorway. "Lacey!" she cried, dropping the groceries on the kitchen island. She was beside her in a heartbeat, assessing the damage. "Oh, Lacey, what have you done?" she asked worriedly.

Lacey attempted to sit up, forcing a smile to her face. The fall had been a jolt, and she wondered, had she damaged her leg? She had her answer when a slice of pain shot through the leg. She ventured a glance at it, reaching a trembling hand toward the leg of her pants. She gently hoisted it up, and then her eyes widened with terror. She saw that she'd somehow managed to jar the pins, one of which now appeared to pierce the leg at an odd, slanting angle. She felt a wave of nausea, and released the pant leg. She took in deep, calming breaths.

"It's okay, Lacey," Millie said, attempting to keep her voice steady. "But I need to get you to the doctor now. He needs to see that leg."

"I'm sure it's all right," she said, hoping it was true.

"I'm calling Robert," Millie said. "Or maybe I should call for an ambulance."

"No, no, please call Robert. I don't think the neighbors would appreciate the commotion of an ambulance." Not to mention, she hated the idea herself.

Millie snatched up the cordless phone and dialed Robert, who answered on the second ring. She filled him in on Lacey's fall, and then hung up the phone. "He'll be here in a couple minutes," Millie assured her. "Should I call Mason?"

"No! I mean, no, I'd rather you didn't." She couldn't bear the thought of him hurrying home on her account. The man needed a break from constant worry about her.

"I don't know," Millie said with a wince. "He won't like it if we don't call him."

Lacey smiled reassuringly, despite the pain in her leg. "I just can't stand the idea of interrupting his conference. It's important to him."

"You're important," Millie said resolutely.

"Well, I appreciate your saying so, but I'm sure my leg is fine. If it turns out I've done serious damage to it . . ."

"You'll let me call him then?"

She nodded. "I promise. But now, I have another call to make."

Millie shook her head sternly. "Not now. It'll have to wait."

She was about to protest when Robert stormed into the

room, his features crunched with worry. "Lacey, what did you do?"

"Fell," she told him. "I'm fine."

"We'll see about that," he said, bending to help her up off the floor. Millie also lent an arm, and she was soon upright again. The couple escorted her to Robert's waiting sedan.

Chapter Nineteen

Well, Lacey, the leg looks okay," Dr. Marks said.

She had just awakened in recovery after the surgical procedure to remove the pins from her leg. The doctor stood beside her hospital bed, gently probing the now contraption-free leg.

"Will you put the cast back on?" she asked, assessing her leg. While it didn't look good, it didn't look too bad. Thanks to Robert, a plastic surgeon had been called to consult with Dr. Marks during the surgery, and had affected a smooth repair to the badly damaged skin.

"We won't put you in a cast, but will rely on a type of splint," he told her.

"Did I do a lot of damage to your repair work when I fell?" she inquired, bracing for his answer.

He shook his head. "Thankfully, no. The bones had already mended nicely, but . . ." He raised a cautionary finger. "You're going to have to take it very easy for a while. I don't want the leg jarred or jostled. You could have done much more serious damage with that fall. You're lucky," he finished.

She nodded. "Can I use crutches?" she asked hopefully.

He shook his head. "Not for a week or two. There is a weak spot in the bone, just above the ankle. When you fell, the pin at the location bent. Again, it could have been far worse, but that bone needs time to heal."

She sighed. She hated the idea of relying on a wheelchair

again. Attempting to look on the bright side, she asked, "Can I go home today?"

He appeared to consider her question. "You can, provided you have someone to help you out there. I cannot stress enough that you need to baby that leg for a week or two."

She sighed. "I'll be careful," she assured him.

"And no more dashing to answer the phone," Robert said as he strode into the room. "Next time, just let the machine get it."

She smiled in his direction. "Pop, thanks for—"

He raised a silencing hand. He knew she was referring to the plastic surgeon. "You're my daughter, Lacey Jane," he said, smiling fondly.

She returned his smile, grateful for the love he had always displayed for her. She couldn't have asked for a better father than Robert. Why hadn't she appreciated him more in the past? She knew the answer. She'd been too focused on herself.

"Lacey, will you let me call Mason?" he asked. "He'll be fit to be tied if he finds out you're hurt and we didn't tell him."

"He'll find out soon enough," she murmured miserably. "Besides, I'm fine."

He sighed. "All right, but you're going to have to explain to him why we didn't call him immediately."

"I will," she promised, "but for now, let's let him have his fun at the conference."

"I'm not sure how much fun he's having," Robert said doubtfully.

A nurse entered the room with Lacey's discharge papers and was wheeling her to Robert's sedan in no time. Soon they were back at Mason's house, where Lacey was once again deposited in his chair.

Robert eyed her speculatively. "What's the plan, Lacey Jane?" he asked.

"The plan," she mused aloud. "The plan keeps changing," she said with a sigh.

"What about that partnership offer?" he said. "Does this situation put a damper on that particular prospect?"

She shrugged. "I don't know. Probably. The fates do seem intent on stalling my decision."

"You can't very well work in that wheelchair," he pointed out. "Maybe it's not meant to be. . . ."

The old Lacey might have railed against the suggestion. Not today. Maybe Robert was right. Maybe Mason was right. Maybe the partnership wasn't for her. Maybe she should simply call Keith and apprise him of her current situation. Surely she couldn't keep postponing the decision—or asking him to wait on her decision. Particularly when there was no telling when she could return to Portland. Dr. Marks had been adamant that she take care with the leg.

"I don't know what I'm going to do," she muttered miserably. "I've never felt this helpless before. I don't like it," she said. "It's not me."

"You're not helpless," Robert said, smiling indulgently. "You're simply indisposed. The leg will heal."

"Yes, but when? And how long can I keep imposing on Mason? He has a life to get back to."

Robert met her gaze. "Why don't you talk to him about that?"

"I have, but he just keeps saying that I'm not imposing and that he's fine with our current arrangement."

He patted her hand. "He is fine with your current arrangement."

"Turns out Mason has the patience of a saint," she murmured drolly. "Who knew?"

"There's a lot you don't know about Mason," Robert said, eyeing her speculatively.

"Such as?"

"Talk to him," Robert said. "Talk to him."

Lacey resolved she would talk to Mason, but not until he returned from his conference. And she also resolved that she wouldn't be the reason he cut it short.

The day after her surgery, she was once again ensconced in his family room, watching television and bored to tears. She'd attempted to reach Melissa, to ask about the message she'd left before, but couldn't get ahold of her. She did leave a message asking that she call her back, but it was all a waiting game now.

Mason had called the evening before. She'd kept the news that she'd reinjured her leg to herself, instead peppering him with questions about the conference. He seemed to be enjoying himself, but said he was eager to return home.

When Millie walked out of Lacey's bedroom, she met her gaze. "You're bored, aren't you?" she asked.

She sighed. "Not much else to be."

"You miss Mason."

She didn't bother denying it.

Suddenly, the doorbell rang and she sat more upright in the chair as Millie hurried to answer it. To her surprise, Donna walked into the room, followed by several members of her grandmother's church.

"Hello," she greeted them, wondering why they'd come. She noticed each held a food item of some sort—from casseroles to desserts.

"We've brought over some food," Donna told her. "We heard about you injuring your leg again. We thought you could freeze most of the food and pop it into the oven when you need it."

"That's so sweet of you," she said. "Would you like to sit down?"

While Donna hurriedly stowed the food in the refrigerator or freezer, the other ladies took seats on the couch and loveseat. Lacey smiled uncertainly their way, glad when Millie dropped onto the arm of her chair. "Isn't this nice, Lacey?" she said.

"It really is," she said. "It's wonderful to have visitors and I can't tell you how much I appreciate the food." She glanced back at the island in the kitchen, which was presently covered in assorted desserts. "Wow, those look great," she enthused over the enticing treats.

"You always had a sweet tooth when you were little," Pastor Wilson's wife said.

Lacey smiled. She couldn't deny it. Anytime the church had a function involving good food, she had hovered around the dessert table, sampling anything that struck her fancy— which was nearly everything.

Suddenly, Mrs. Wilson laughed. "I'll never forget the time you polished off half a chocolate cake," she said, meeting her eyes. "You couldn't have been more than seven, and you loved chocolate."

"Still do," she admitted with a smile.

"And there was the one church picnic where Lacey was determined to sample every dessert," another woman commented, and then met her gaze. "You meticulously cut a tiny slice of each dessert, until you had a veritable rainbow of dessert items on your plate."

"I remember that," she said, chuckling.

"How about a slice of cake now?" Millie suggested as she rose to cut slices for everyone.

Lacey's eyes lit up. "Sounds good."

The ladies chuckled, and she joined their laughter. It was

odd. This stroll down memory lane wasn't so painful. In fact, the memories were good ones. How had she forgotten the pleasant memories? she wondered. There had been plenty of those during her time in Westover. Rennie had seen to it, as had Robert, and even Mason.

She chuckled. "One time Mason smuggled me more desserts than any kid should have eaten in one sitting," she remembered. "I got sick and he got in trouble."

"He was always willing to risk punishment where you were concerned," Mrs. Wilson said, smiling at the memory. "Half the time, he fessed up when you were the guilty party."

Lacey winced. "I know. But he wised up soon enough."

"Not too soon," Donna observed with a grin. "If memory serves, it took him years to declare that you had cooties."

One of the ladies, Alice Dupont, laughed. "Most of the little boys in this town were smitten with Lacey," she said. "My Johnny was fit to be tied when Mason told the whole grammar school she was his girlfriend."

"Mason did that?" she asked with surprise.

Donna nodded her head vigorously. "He certainly did. He told everybody he was going to marry you someday and that they'd better steer clear."

Mrs. Dupont nodded in agreement. "I remember, because Johnny came home and asked his daddy for a sword."

"What did he want with a sword?" Millie asked.

"He wanted to challenge Mason to a duel."

Lacey shook her head. "I have no memory of any of that."

"That's because you wouldn't give those boys the time of day," Donna said. "You said you were going to have a career someday and didn't need, as you put it, 'no husband.' "

"You were such a little character," the pastor's wife said, smiling softly.

"Lacey," Mrs. Dupont spoke up, "do you remember one day

at church when you marched right up to me—you must have been about eight and I was around eight months pregnant with my fifth? Anyway, I had four boys at that point, and you stopped dead still in front of me and said, 'That's a girl you got cookin' in there.'"

"Hey!" Donna said, rising to her feet and spreading her arms wide. "Uh, Lacey, over here! Am I not your best friend in this town? Are you holding out on me?"

She chuckled. "It's a girl you've got cookin' in there."

Donna dropped onto the couch and laughed good-naturedly. "Really?"

Lacey shrugged. "I hope so," she said with a wince.

"I guess your gender-divining powers have left you," Millie said with a chuckle.

Lacey turned to Millie. "I didn't remember I had any." She turned to Mrs. Dupont. "You did have a girl that time, didn't you?"

She nodded vigorously. "My one and only. If you'll remember, I asked you your opinion with each subsequent pregnancy."

"How many children do you have?" Millie asked with interest.

"Seven," she told her, but turned back to Lacey. "Anyway, each time I asked you your opinion about the sex of the baby, you'd just shake your head sadly and mutter, 'It's a doggone boy.' And you were right—every time."

The ladies visited for a while, until Mrs. Wilson announced it was time to leave. "We'd planned to come see you when you first arrived in town," she said, "and had planned to bring by food then, but Mason . . ." Suddenly, she paused, as if she'd said too much.

"Mason what?" she asked, watching her curiously.

"Well, he was so worried about you, he didn't want anyone to disturb you," Mrs. Wilson informed her.

"Protective as a grizzly bear where she's concerned," Millie said.

"Anyway, we wanted to say how much we've missed you—our Little Lacey Jane," Mrs. Wilson said. "When you were little, you lit up this town. I don't think anybody could resist that impish grin of yours."

She felt a wave of nostalgia wash over her. It was sweet of the ladies to come, and bearing food. It had actually been fun reminiscing about old times. These ladies seemed to genuinely care about her—or at least had cared about her when she was little. How had she not realized that?

"Thank you all for coming," she said. "You've brightened my day."

And given me something to think about. But she didn't say those words out loud.

Chapter Twenty

The next morning, Lacey placed a call to Melissa. Again, she couldn't reach her and left a message. She was dying to know what she had learned about her father.

She sat in Mason's family room, resisting the urge to make a grab for her crutches. They were propped against the nearby loveseat and she watched them yearningly.

Millie saw the longing look in her eyes and promptly moved them. "Don't even think about it," she warned.

"You read me pretty well," Lacey observed.

"Well, it wasn't exactly hard, being as you were staring at those crutches like they were a piece of chocolate . . . or . . ." She giggled.

"Or what?"

"Or Mason."

She gasped. "I do not stare at Mason as if he were a piece of chocolate," she insisted.

Millie laughed and raised her hands in surrender. "Just saying. Hey, how about a piece of chocolate cake?"

"I'm going to be as big as a house," Lacey said, but grinned gleefully. "Okay."

Millie chuckled again. "Cake on the way."

She was just passing her a slice when Mason strode into the family room. Lacey glanced at him in surprise, her eyes indicating the pleasure she felt to see him. He noticed.

"You missed me," he said smugly, and then grinned. "Good, because I missed you too."

She smiled, and was almost embarrassed by the warm feeling that traveled from the top of her head to the tips of her toes. "I didn't expect you until later this evening," she said.

"Today was a sort of final meet and greet. I didn't stick around for it."

"Mason . . . ," she scolded. "You should have."

He ignored her and turned to Millie instead. "Hi, Millie. How have things been?"

Her eyes widened and she bid a hasty retreat from the room. Lacey realized she likely didn't want to be the one to mention her latest injury.

"What was that about?" Mason inquired, his features puzzled.

"Oh, nothing. So tell me all about the conference."

"It was fine," he muttered off-handedly, still watching after Millie with a frown.

"I want to see your plaque," she said eagerly.

"No plaque," he told her. "A trophy instead."

"Trophies are better than plaques anyway," she told him. "Well, let me see it."

"Later," he said, smiling into her eyes as he dropped into the nearby loveseat. "So, have you been keeping busy?"

She weighed the question with a side-to-side tilt of her head. "Trying to. Can't do much with this leg."

"How's it feeling?" He rose up and tugged at the throw blanket that currently covered her leg. His eyes widened when he noticed the original cast was gone. "What . . . ?"

She smiled reassuringly. "Dr. Marks removed the pins," she told him cheerfully.

"But you weren't scheduled for a doctor's appointment this week," he said, furrowing his brow.

"Well, I had a tiny mishap," she admitted, and then braced for the explosion. Curiously, none came.

"Lacey," he said, almost in a whisper, "what happened?"

"Nothing really," she assured him. "I took a tumble and one of the pins bent and . . ."

He made a mortified face. "A pin bent?"

"Well, yeah, but it's okay. I have to stay off crutches for a week or two, but then I'll be good to go."

"Good to go? What do you mean, good to go? You're not going anywhere," he declared.

"Well, I'm not going anywhere in the immediate future, but I will be going . . . soon. I mean, come on, it's time." As she said the words, Lacey realized she didn't really want to go anywhere. The very realization caused a mortified glow to stain her cheeks. What was happening to her? She was a career woman, with dreams and ambitions, yet . . .

Mason rose from the chair and raked a hand through his hair. "Yeah, okay, Lacey. You're going then? Back to Portland. Am I right?"

"Well, I . . ."

He threw his hands in the air. "I can't believe you're even considering going back at this point. Lacey, come on. You need to stay here. Your family is here. I'm . . . here."

She watched him, mouth agape. What was he saying? She opened her mouth to speak, but promptly clamped it shut. What should she say? What could she say?

He sighed. "I have to go. I'll see you tonight."

She watched after his retreating figure. Why was he so upset?

Mason called hours later. It was late evening, and Lacey was relieved to hear his voice. She was about to tell him as much when he said briskly, "Something's come up. I have to go out of town for a day or two."

"Mason, I . . . ," she began, but he hurriedly got off the phone before she could finish her thought. She could only stare at the receiver in her hand. She had been so eager for him to come home.

She felt confused, uncertain. Mason didn't want her to leave—she knew that. And in truth, she didn't want to go. But she had to do something—make a move of some type. She couldn't live with him forever. But she knew, deep down, she couldn't go back to Portland and her former job either. Maybe it *was* true—you can't go home again.

With a deep, shoring breath, she dialed Keith's home number. He answered after several rings. "Keith, I'm afraid I won't be coming back to the firm in any capacity," she told him in a rush, before she could change her mind.

"But, Lacey . . ."

"I can't ask the firm to wait on me any longer. I'm afraid I've reinjured my leg, so it's hard to say when I'll finally be back in good form."

"Ah, I'm sorry," he said. "We're going to miss you. Will you be staying in Westover?"

She considered the question and sighed heavily. "I . . . don't think so."

Later, in bed, Lacey tossed and turned, her mind plagued with thoughts of her future. What should she do?

Should she head back to Portland and open a small law office? It was an idea—something she'd considered in the past. She knew the pace would be hectic initially as she set up a practice, but she would soon experience ebbs and flows in business activity as she established a clientele. She also knew she'd have a level of control over her own work life that she hadn't had as an up-and-comer at the large Portland firm.

Of course, until her leg significantly improved, she wouldn't be in any condition to open a law office. She just didn't have the mobility to do what needed doing. That held true for Rennie's house too. She had hoped to be able to complete any repairs to the house. Heck, she'd hoped to be able to move in, despite the broken leg.

She groaned loudly. Who knew an injury could so dramatically alter her life? And she was more fortunate than most. At least her job wasn't as physical as another might have been.

Finally, finally, she drifted off to sleep. She woke early, and didn't feel particularly rested. She forced herself up and called for Millie, who had already arrived. She hurried into the room. "Morning, Lacey," she said cheerfully.

She attempted a smile, but couldn't quite pull it off.

"Rough night?" Millie asked, frowning.

"I had a lot on my mind," she told her friend.

"You have a lot to think about, huh?"

Lacey nodded and smoothed a hand through her hair. "I need to decide my future," she said miserably. "I can't keep relying on the kindness of others—like you," she added.

Millie smiled. "Robert considers you a daughter, you know. And Mason, well, he's just plain in love with you." Before she could respond, Millie continued, "And I consider you a dear friend."

Lacey returned her warm smile. "Right back at you. But as far as Mason being in love with me . . . I don't think so. He probably considers me a royal pain in the butt," she said with a laugh. "He always did."

Millie chuckled. "He wants you to stay in Westover. For that matter, he wants you to stay in this house."

She shook her head. "No, he's just one of the good guys. He feels a curious responsibility for me, and for the life of me, I really can't figure out why. I mean, it's not like we're kids anymore."

"He . . . loves . . . you . . . Lacey," Millie intoned. "For heaven's sake, can't you see that?"

Lacey didn't respond. What could she say?

Millie helped her get ready for the day, and then helped her into the wheelchair. Lacey checked the time. It was after eight. She hurriedly dialed Melissa's work number, and felt relief when she heard a real voice. Unfortunately, it wasn't Mason's assistant who answered.

She recognized the voice. It belonged to the woman she had heard Melissa talking to that day at the sheriff's office.

"Hello, this is Lacey Karr. May I speak to Melissa, please?"

She felt herself stiffen when the woman informed her, "Melissa has gone out of town with the sheriff. I don't know when they plan to return."

If she had managed to find her voice, she might have asked where the couple had gone. But, she realized, it was none of her business.

She replaced the phone on the hook and then inhaled deeply, to slow her pounding heart. Mason and Melissa had gone off together. Perhaps it was work related, but . . .

It was clear Melissa had feelings for him. She had said as much that day Lacey had overheard her gossiping. Did Mason care for her too? Had the two been involved? Had her arrival in town, and subsequent injury, thrown a monkey wrench into what had been a budding romance?

She sighed heavily. She'd become a major pain for Mason. She'd moved into his house and had thoroughly disrupted his life. She owed him, and more than a debt of gratitude for all that he had done for her. What she owed him most, she realized, was the gift of his life back.

She hurriedly dialed her best friend from Portland, Laura. Her bubbly friend picked up on the first ring. "It's about time you called me," she scolded. "Geez, Lacey, ever hear of charging your cell phone? If I didn't hear something from you soon, I was going to send the cavalry."

"I'm sorry."

"I guess I can forgive you. I'm sure you've been busy. How's life in Westover? I'm coming to see you soon, by the way."

She smiled at her friend's cheerful declaration, and then sobered. "Hey, do you think you could make it really soon? I . . ."

"What is it?" Laura prompted.

"Do you think you could come today?"

"What's going on, Lacey?" she asked with concern.

She quickly filled her in on Rennie's passing, her own accident, and her current living arrangements.

"Wow," Laura said. "I'm so sorry about Rennie. And why didn't you get in touch with me about your accident? I can hardly stand to think about what might have been. . . ." She paused for several long seconds before continuing, "And yes, of course I'll come for you. I'll leave here in ten. But are you sure you want to leave? Should you discuss it with Mason first? From what you've told me, it's apparent he cares about you."

"Why would I discuss it with him?" she said. "He doesn't know what's good for him, anyway. He's feels this sense of responsibility for me that originated somewhere in our childhood. I think it's best I make the decision and stick with it. It's time he got his life back."

"If you say so," Laura muttered. "I can say, I'm glad you're coming home. I've really missed you. You're staying with me, by the way."

"Thank you. This leg has really put a damper on my ability to make plans, but thankfully, I'm on the mend now."

"Hey, will you return to your old job?" she asked. "Keith left a message on my machine while I was away, asking that I wield whatever influence I have with you and talk you into returning to the firm."

Lacey considered her friend's words. "You know, he's called several times, and actually offered me a partnership, but . . ."

"But what? Wait. Isn't that great news?"

"The truth is, I don't know what I want anymore."

"Could your . . . Mason James . . . have anything to do with that?"

She sighed. "Hey, how was Hawaii?" she asked, changing the subject.

"So much for subtle shifts in conversation," Laura commented. "Okay, I'll let you get away with it. Hawaii was great. I hated to come home."

"I know what you mean," she murmured.

Suddenly, the prospect of leaving Westover felt like . . . *leaving* home.

Chapter Twenty-one

My car won't start," Laura declared over the phone a half hour later. "I don't know what's wrong with it."

Lacey sighed, and then offered her friend the name of a good mechanic she had relied on more than once in the past.

"As soon as I get my car running, I'll be on my way," Laura told her.

"I'm sorry," she said. "I shouldn't expect you to drop everything and drive all the way from Portland to Westover."

"Lacey, I don't mind," Laura assured her. "I can't wait to see you. I'll get there as soon as I can."

After Laura promised to keep her posted on the condition of the car, they signed off. Lacey subsided into the comfortable recliner. It looked like she wasn't going anywhere for a while. She found herself staring at the clock, wondering, was Mason enjoying his weekend?

She felt a twinge of jealousy when she contemplated the implications of Melissa's accompanying him on the trip. What *did* it mean?

She feared the worst, and then wondered, what was the worst? Forcing herself to look honestly at the situation, she realized the worst was that Mason and Melissa were involved. The idea bothered her. She forced herself to admit the reason it bothered her. She loved Mason.

When had it happened? Had she always loved him, and been

too stubborn to realize it? Or had she fallen for him during this recent visit? Admittedly, she'd seen sides to him she hadn't seen, or been willing to see, in the past. He had many admirable qualities, not the least of which was that he was a good and decent man.

She continued to contemplate her feelings for him over the remainder of the weekend. Did he love her too?

The instant the possibility entered her mind, she envisioned Mason and Melissa together and couldn't dismiss the possibility of the two being involved. Maybe having Lacey around had given clarity to his feelings for Melissa. Maybe having her around had shown him that the other woman was the right one for him.

Lacey groaned aloud. Why was she so stubborn and combative? And why was she so indecisive of late? She couldn't seem to make a decision to save her life. What *did* she want?

Or, perhaps the better question was, *who* did she want? And suddenly, with a clarity she hadn't felt in a very long time, she knew the answer. Mason.

Hours later, she was tipped back in the recliner, an arm thrown across her face, when he strode into the family room. "Lacey?"

She started, and then dropped her arm. Having him suddenly appear felt as if she'd somehow conjured him up. "Hi," she murmured numbly.

"Hi," he said, watching her curiously.

"How was your weekend?" she asked.

"Give me a minute to change and I'll tell you all about it," he said, and then headed upstairs to his bedroom.

Lacey eased into the chair, mentally shoring herself for what he might soon tell her. Myriad possibilities entered her mind, and by the time he returned, her face was rife with concern.

"Hey, are you all right?" he asked, sitting down on the nearby loveseat.

"Fine," she assured him. "Did you and Melissa have a nice weekend?"

Mason shook his head as if to clear it. "What?"

Lacey didn't immediately register that she'd actually voiced the words that had entered her mind.

"What did you say?" he persisted.

"Oh, uh, nothing. I was just wondering about your weekend."

He sat down again, his eyes pinned on her face. He smiled suddenly. "You thought I went out of town with Melissa?" He shook his head. "I mean, I did go out of town with her, or rather, she accompanied me." He shook his head. "That didn't come out right either. What I'm trying to say is, she accompanied me to Woodville, since we finally got a good lead on your father."

Lacey sat up straight in the chair. "You did? Why didn't you tell me before you left?"

"Because I knew you'd insist on accompanying me, which, had you not reinjured your leg, you could have done."

"I could have gone despite this leg," she insisted.

He raised a conciliatory hand. "Look, Melissa went with me, since two heads are better than one. While I was talking to—"

"Who?" she asked eagerly.

"While I was talking to your father's mother's former neighbor—and best friend—Melissa took a side trip to the college."

She watched him, eyes shining. "What did you find out?"

He leaned forward in the chair, his hands clasped together and his eyes pinned on her face. "It's like you figured. Your mother didn't want to disappoint Rennie, so . . ."

"Go on," she urged.

"Okay," he said with a laugh. "Anyway, your mother met your father when she was a freshman in college. The two dated briefly, fell in love, and got married."

"Okay," she said. "And then what?"

"Well, according to your grandmother's neighbor—"

"And former best friend . . ."

He nodded. "Right, and if what this woman says is true, and I believe it is, your mother decided to drop out of college to work, in order to help your father through school."

"And she became pregnant with me," she mused, struggling to sort out the time frame in her head.

"That's right. Anyway, your father was enrolled in the college's ROTC program, and when he finished school, he enlisted in the military. Your mother tried to make it on her own for a while after he went off to basic training and was later deployed, but she apparently had a rough go of it."

"Okay, so she didn't come home immediately after my father was deployed?"

He shook his head. "No. Apparently, she was so afraid of disappointing Rennie that she delayed coming home."

"What made her change her mind?" Lacey wondered aloud. "And where did she live?"

He leaned forward and clasped her hand. "She lived with your father's mother—your grandmother."

Lacey attempted to digest everything he was telling her. "Is my grandmother alive?" she asked. It would be wonderful to meet her.

He shook his head. "I'm afraid not. The night your mother raced out of Rennie's house, it was actually this neighbor that I spoke to who placed the phone call you've always wondered about."

"Why did she make the call?" she asked, watching his face intently.

"Your grandmother had had a heart attack, and it was bad, Lacey. Her friend was trying to reach Jessie in time for her to return in order to say good-bye to your grandmother."

"Did she make it in time?" she asked softly. She knew what it felt like to arrive too late to say good-bye.

He shook his head sadly. "I'm afraid not. Your grandmother died as Jessie was driving to the hospital, and as you know, she . . ."

"Didn't make it."

"Apparently, Jessie and your father's mother were very close, particularly after . . ."

"After what?"

"After your father was killed overseas. His death is what prompted Jessie to finally come home."

She gasped, and then leaned back in the chair. So, her father and grandmother were dead. What about her grandfather? She figured he must be dead too, since Mason made no mention of him.

She attempted to focus. "How did my father die?"

Mason squeezed her hand. "He was killed during an embassy bombing in Beirut. Apparently, he died a hero. He'd been wounded, but despite his injury, he attempted to help others to safety. Were it not for a second assault on the embassy, he might have lived—and the others."

She sighed loudly. She couldn't find the words. She finally had the answers she'd been seeking for so many years. Jessie hadn't left her behind. She had intended to come back all along. She had simply hurried off to tend to her father's mother, who had had a heart attack. Had she not been killed in a car accident that awful night, she would have returned and Lacey would have grown up with a mother.

"Mason, you're sure about all this, right? Is there any doubt this information is true?"

He shook his head. "I believe it's true, Lacey. The woman I talked to, her name is Agnes Morgan. She and your grandmother, Lydia Sanders, by the way, were friends for many, many years. Agnes had a son who went to school with your father. They were best friends growing up. Agnes had the pictures to prove it."

She frowned. "I wonder why Agnes didn't try to reach Rennie. . . . Did she wonder what had happened to me?"

He sighed. "Initially, she was grief-stricken by the loss of her friend, and then later, Jessie. She said she was out of commission for several months. Also, she assumed that since you weren't in the car with your mother, you were safe. In fairness to her, she didn't know Rennie's name, so tracking her would have been difficult. She did say she made inquiries, but ultimately gave up."

"I'd like to meet her."

He nodded. "Of course. As soon as your leg permits."

She nodded, satisfied. She felt as if a weight had been lifted. As hopeful as she'd been that she might find living family members, she was grateful to finally know the truth behind her arrival in Westover, as well as the story behind what had happened to her mother and father. Her parents had loved each other. Her mother had apparently forged a loving relationship with her mother-in-law, and . . . Jessie had finally come home.

Apparently, Jessie had realized how much she needed and missed her own mother. And now Lacey also knew why no relatives had attempted to locate her after Jessie had died. There was no one left.

Mason watched her face. He gave her a moment to process. "It's a lot to take in, isn't it?" he said softy.

She nodded. "Yes."

"Do you need a break? We can talk more later."

She shook her head. "I'm all right."

"Good," he said with a soft, rueful smile. "Because you and I apparently need to clarify a few things."

"Oh?" she said, meeting his eyes. "What things?"

"So you thought Melissa and I . . ." His words trailed off.

She shrugged. "Well, yeah. Obviously, the woman cares about you."

"We're co-workers, Lacey," he said, scrubbing a hand across his jaw. "I've never thought about her like that."

"Good," she muttered beneath her breath, and then glanced up with alarm. Had she really spoken aloud again?

He chuckled. "Are *we* good?" he asked.

She met his eyes. She wasn't exactly certain what he meant by the question. Her mind was still reeling from the information he'd given her about her family. She wasn't sure this was the right time for the conversation they were apparently about to have, but he had given her an out previously and she hadn't taken him up on it. She shook her head to clear it and watched him curiously.

"What do you mean, Mason?"

"You don't know?"

She shrugged apologetically.

He rose from the loveseat and strode a few steps away, and then returned. "Lacey, I . . ."

Suddenly, a loud, booming voice came from the foyer. "Where's that son of mine?"

Mason ran a frustrated hand through his hair and shook his head. "In here, Pop!"

Robert entered the room and glanced between Mason and Lacey. "What's going on?"

Neither answered, and Robert spoke. "I came to see your plaque, son."

"Trophy," Mason and Lacey said in unison.

"Well, trophy then," Robert said jovially.

"Later, Pop," Mason said, shooting his father a look of daggers.

Robert didn't get the hint. "Come on. It's not every day my son is chosen Law Enforcement Officer of the Year."

"Pop," Mason growled, and tossed him his keys. "It's in the truck."

Robert snatched the keys from the air and strode out of the house. Mason watched after him briefly. "He's always had lousy timing."

He glanced back at Lacey and saw the fatigue on her face. As much as he wanted to talk to her, to clear some things up, he realized his timing was off too.

"It's getting late. You should probably get some sleep."

She nodded. "Maybe so."

The next morning, Lacey rose with Millie's help. She hadn't slept much, having spent much of the night contemplating the information Mason had brought home with him. It was good to have answers, although she would have preferred a happy ending involving a reunion with family.

Millie wheeled her into the family room and to the breakfast nook, where Mason was eating a bowl of cereal. He rose to situate the wheelchair at the table.

"Are you sure you won't be needing me today, Mason?" Millie asked.

"No, we're fine," he assured her. "You go enjoy a day off."

"She needs one after hanging out with me," Lacey said with a smile at her friend.

"Hey, you're no trouble at all," Millie informed them cheerfully, and then glanced at Mason. "Are you taking a day off, then?"

He nodded. "Yep, I am."

With a good-bye, Millie hurried off, while Mason turned his attention to Lacey. "How are you feeling?" he asked, appearing to brace for her answer.

"I'm good," she told him, realizing it was true. It had been good to hear that she was the product of two people who loved each other, rather than learning she'd been unwanted, or that her mother had been involved with someone who hadn't been good to her or for her. "I am good," she said, meeting his eyes. "Thank you, Mason, for everything."

He smiled. "Anytime. And now, about what we were going to discuss last night, before Pop showed up . . ."

"Yes?"

Suddenly, the doorbell rang. Mason checked his watch. "Who can that be so early?"

He rose to answer the door and soon walked into the family room behind Laura. He wore a befuddled expression on his face. "Your friend is here," he informed her, unnecessarily.

Lacey hastily made introductions, and then Laura turned to her. "I know I should have called, but I could tell you were eager to get home, so . . ."

Lacey glanced at Mason's face in time to see the look of surprise. He snared her gaze. "You're . . . leaving?"

"Well, I . . ."

Before she could finish, he shook his head and made as if to leave. He paused only briefly to nod at Laura. "It's nice to have met you," he said, and then strode from the room.

"I'm sorry," Laura said with a wince. "You obviously haven't told him you intend to leave Westover yet."

"No, but it's . . . okay," she assured her. "You're a good friend for coming."

"I should have called . . ."

Lacey didn't respond, but instead watched after Mason. She heard the front door close with a bang.

Chapter Twenty-two

A re you sure?" Laura asked for the umpteenth time.

Lacey nodded with certainty. "I'm sure. I may be too late, but I'm sure."

"Okay, here it is," Laura said, passing her the shirt she had picked up at a nearby store. "Red and white with a number twelve on it. Did you manage to get ahold of Mason? He's gorgeous, by the way."

She nodded distractedly. "He's much more than a handsome face," she said, hoping desperately she hadn't ruined things—hoping desperately she hadn't misread him and wasn't about to make a fool of herself.

"So you called him?" Laura asked.

She nodded. "He didn't sound happy, but he agreed to come home to talk. He should be back here any minute. Apparently, he went by the station to catch up on some paperwork."

He walked into the family room moments later, nodded at Laura, and then made a beeline for the refrigerator.

Laura bid a hasty retreat. "I'm going to check out your town, Lacey," she called over her shoulder.

Mason turned toward Lacey when he heard the door close behind her friend. "Your town? *Your* town? That'll be the day," he grumbled.

She bit back a smile at seeing his uncharacteristic surly side. Besides, if things went as planned, Westover *would* be her town, and . . . Westover might very well have a new attorney.

"*Your town,*" he muttered again. "Yeah, right."

"Mason, can we talk?"

"Sure," he said mock-agreeably. "I'm here. Let's talk." He closed the refrigerator, left the kitchen, and headed for the family room. He dropped onto the loveseat and watched her expectantly. "So, when do you leave?"

"I . . ."

"Just so you know," he cut in before she could answer, "I think you're being ridiculous. Your leg is messed up again, and you think you can go back to Portland and pick up a hectic lifestyle without doing additional damage to it. If you ask me . . ."

"Mason . . ."

"I can't even fathom you're thinking you're okay to make a five-hour drive with that leg. . . ."

"Mason . . ."

"And I'll never understand why you hate this town so much," he added for good measure. "These people love you, despite what you think, Lacey Jane. They care about you, but you just can't see that, can you?"

"Mason . . ."

"And what about me? I think I've made it pretty clear how I feel about you."

"Mason . . ."

"It's not every day I move a woman into my house, you know." He rose and began pacing.

"Mason . . ."

"And did you give any thought to how Pop is going to feel about your leaving?"

She realized she wasn't going to get a word in. Mason had suddenly become as talkative as she'd ever seen him. She realized that sometimes actions do speak louder than words. His actions certainly had. He had taken her in when she was down and out—had altered his life for her—and had done it all cheerfully and . . . lovingly.

She reached for the T-shirt she'd stuffed between the arm of the chair and the seat cushion. Before he could speak again, she tossed the T-shirt to him. He caught it easily and stared at it curiously.

"What's this?" he asked. He snapped the shirt, exposing the number on the back. "It's my number," he murmured.

Lacey watched him expectantly, her heart in her throat. Was it too late?

A slow smile spread across his face. "Does this mean what I think—what I . . . hope it means?"

She nodded again. "I realized a few things."

"Such as?" he prompted softly.

"Give me the shirt back."

He stepped closer and handed her the shirt, which she promptly, but awkwardly, slipped into.

"What have you realized, Lacey?" he asked, an expectant look on his face.

She met his gaze and smiled. "Well, I realized I love you, Mason. I . . . think I always have."

"Well, it's about time, Lacey Jane," he said with relief. "Because I know I've always loved you."

He laughed with wonder, then, before leaning toward her and claiming her lips in a kiss. Suddenly, he rose, spun, and jogged from the room. He returned a moment later, clutching something small in his hand.

She watched him curiously. "What is it, Mason?"

"If you're willing to wear the shirt, I wonder . . ." He held out the sparkling engagement ring for her to see. "Will you marry me, Lacey Jane?" he asked, his smile wide and his eyes glistening with hopeful anticipation.

An answering, radiant smile lit her face and she could only nod yes. He slipped the ring on her finger and then took both her hands in his. "You're home," he said softly, triumphantly. "Finally."

"Finally," she agreed, "I'm home."